THE MYSTERY
OF DREAR HOUSE

Virginia Hamilton

THE MYSTERY OF DREAR HOUSE

The Conclusion of the
Dies Drear Chronicle

GREENWILLOW BOOKS
New York

15 14 13 12 11

Library of Congress Cataloging-in-Publication Data

Hamilton, Virginia. The mystery of Drear House.
Sequel to: The house of Dies Drear.
Summary: A black family living in the house of
long-dead abolitionist Dies Drear must decide what to
do with his stupendous treasure, hidden for one
hundred years in a cavern near their home.
[1. Afro-Americans—Fiction]   I. Title.
PZ7.H1828My   1987   [Fic]   86-9829
ISBN 0-688-04026-8

Typeset by Fisher Composition, Inc.

THE MYSTERY
OF DREAR HOUSE

1

The cool days of October descended upon the region. Thomas Small and his papa had taken to the woods to hunt or hike for hours on the hill above the bleak house of Dies Drear. But then, suddenly, it turned cold. Mr. Small had little free time from teaching at the college. On weekends he cataloged the wealth that had belonged to the long-dead abolitionist Dies Eddington Drear. There was a stupendous treasure hidden for a hundred years in a secret cavern within the hillside. Thomas left his rifle at home. He spent the time playing with his little brothers, or by himself, or with his friend Pesty Darrow.

Today he had on a sweater and his fleece-lined jacket over it. The air was brisk. The Drear house seen from the hilltop reminded him of a giant crow frozen on its nest. He wasn't sure yet whether he liked living in that house. He was usually on his guard. Sometimes he felt something strange was near.

Something unseen but listening behind the walls, he thought. He wasn't afraid, just wary whenever he was in the house by himself.

Scaring away mean neighbors, Darrow men, before they had the chance to discover the treasure hadn't rid him of the feeling either. But what was the use of worrying? It was his papa's dream to live in a house that had been a station on the Underground Railroad.

Pesty Darrow was with him today. They'd become friends even though she was a Darrow. Darrows had adopted her when she was an infant. Thomas supposed she was loyal to them since they were the only family she'd known.

She's loyal to us, too, he thought, and to Mr. Pluto.

Mr. Pluto had been the caretaker of the Drear house until the Smalls moved in eight months ago. Old Pluto lived in a cave on the other side of the hill. He and Pesty had kept the secret of the great cavern from everyone. Pesty had known about the secret treasure long before Thomas had. She'd kept it from her brothers and her father, even from her youngest brother, Macky, who wasn't as mean or sour as the others.

But how long can she be loyal to two sets of folk who are like day is to night? Thomas wondered. How long before she makes a slip or the older Darrow men figure out there is treasure deep under the hillside?

Darrows had been hunting for hidden treasure in the maze of underground slave escape tunnels of the region's hills for generations.

Papa's worried they will get bold again, Thomas thought, and try some way to get us off Drear lands. He's afraid there might be cave-ins, too.

"Be quicker if we use the backyard of Drear house," Pesty said.

Thomas had to smile. She was talking about the quick way to her home. Whenever they were out tramping together, she would want Thomas to come see her brother. Every now and then she told Macky, "Mr. Thomas wants to see *you*." Macky snorted and said, "Don't you call no boy mister, Pesty. He's just Thomas, like I am just Macky."

Thomas was careful not to be seen by Darrow men out in the open close to their property. He might overstep their boundary and give them a clear excuse to chase him or to cross the Drear boundary.

Instead of the Drear backyard, he took the longer, out-of-the-way route over the hill because he did want to run into Macky in the woods. He had a vague hope that they might still get to know each other. After school he would see Macky going off in the trees. Lately it seemed that Macky allowed Thomas to catch up with him, almost, before he sauntered away.

Today it had started snowing again. Light snows came now one after the other to the hillside, to the woods and all the land.

"You be glad your grandmom is coming?" Pesty said. "Mr. Pluto told me she was."

"Well, she's not my grandmom," Thomas said as they tramped smartly single file. "She's my great-grand-mother Jeffers. First name is Rhetty. And she's coming to stay. I'm glad of it, too."

"Is she where you used to be?" Pesty asked.

"In North Carolina, yes," he said.

"Do you miss her?"

"Well, it won't feel right here until we're all together again," he said.

"Does she know about the house of Dies Drear?" Pesty asked.

"Pesty, you haven't told anyone about the you-know-what, have you?" he said, meaning the cavern of treas-ure.

"No!" she answered.

"Not even Macky. No one?"

"No!" she said. "I haven't told a soul. I wouldn't." But she sounded anxious. Her voice whined uncer-tainly.

What was it about Pesty lately? Something Thomas

couldn't put his finger on. They were together so much, and he thought he knew her well.

On weekends they often helped his father and old Pluto in the great cavern, where they polished the priceless glass. Pesty, who had taken care of the glass from the time she was five or six, suddenly had butterfingers. She'd dropped a glass spoon and a rare nineteenth-century bottle. Both had smashed on the cavern floor.

Now Thomas made a zigzag trail around trees. Snowflakes slapped thinly, like tiny footsteps around them. He was heading east toward the Darrow- and Carr-owned parts of the woods. Carr people had been friendly when Thomas's family first arrived. Their land bordered Darrow's to the south. They bordered Drear lands on Drear's southeast corner. Darrow land was right by Drear lands, bordering them on Darrow's north and west.

Thomas had been thinking so hard he hadn't noticed that Pesty's footsteps had stopped. He recognized an absence suddenly, and he felt lonely for his great-grandmother and the high mountains of home.

Tired of these long, flat days, he thought. His brothers, Billy and Buster, were too small yet to roam with him.

All at once a voice came out of the trees: "You never can figure when a good day for huntin' will come."

Thomas went cold inside.

"Where's your gun at, friend?" the voice continued. "Tell you one thing, this sure is not a day for huntin' in the woods."

It came to Thomas whom the voice belonged to. He'd wished for this day all these months. There stood M. C. Darrow, called Mac or Macky, the youngest Darrow.

Pesty was nowhere to be seen. She led me here, Thomas was thinking.

He and Mac Darrow gazed at each other. They both stood in fog to their ankles; it made them appear to be floating just above the gound.

Friend or foe? Thomas thought vaguely. Neither one of them smiled.

2

Mac Darrow stood among trees on Darrow land just beyond where Drear lands lined up against it. There was a great old maple tree right on the Drear property line. It had an iron spike deep in the tree trunk, a sure mark of a boundary.

Mac Darrow had grown bigger over the months. Thomas grew lean and wiry and not overly tall yet. But Mac Darrow had grown burly, looking older than his fifteen years. Macky admired Thomas, Thomas could tell in one swift judgment.

After all, Thomas thought, we were smart, Papa, me and Pesty and Mr. Pluto's son and Mr. Pluto, scaring his brothers. They never knew Pesty was there.

But Macky wasn't a part of the Darrows's trying to steal, Thomas went on. They didn't even know what they were after. Just something the old grandfather Darrow came to believe was his. I guess they learned there might be riches somewhere on Drear property from word of mouth handed down from long ago.

Slowly, cautiously, Thomas floated nearer to Macky and Darrow land.

He sighed inwardly and thought: One of the slaves or Indians hiding in the great cavern the night Dies Drear died had to be an ancestor of Macky and his brothers. That had been more than a hundred years ago. Probably an Indian, Thomas mused.

He and Mac Darrow stood watching each other. Every now and then a seeping gray flow of mist would come out of nowhere to ride Macky's shoulders. Then Mac Darrow would appear to be moving.

Wasn't Macky's father's name River? Thomas wondered. Yes, name of River Lewis. And his grandfather was River Swift. One ancester was River Thames. And one of Macky's brothers was River Ross. Probably part Indian, at least.

All was still in the woods. Snowflakes, slapping and scraping thinly. And trees, dark and dripping, unmoved by the excitement Thomas felt at seeing Macky up close. The two of them, alone together after so long.

Thomas glided through the snow, not lifting his feet out of it until he had reached the old maple. There he stopped and leaned against the tree trunk. Macky hadn't moved, being, as he was, at the edge of his family land.

"What are you doing out here?" Thomas called. They were maybe fifteen, twenty feet apart. His voice sounded flat and heavy to him.

"Just . . . out here," Macky said. "Huntin', like I thought you was until I saw you got no gun."

"Oh," said Thomas. "Well. Did you catch anything?"

"Guess you didn't hear what I said before," Macky said.

"What was that?"

"That this ain't a day for man nor beast. For huntin' nothin'."

"Oh," Thomas said.

"You can see the trails of them beasts, though," Macky said. Shyly he looked down and to the side, not quite able to meet Thomas's gaze. "You want to come over, follow the trails?" Said so softly Thomas almost missed it.

Thomas thought about going over. Oh, he wanted to. But he had to say, finally, "I can't come over there."

"Well, you might could, anytime you wanted," Macky

said. "Nobody over here's gonna stop you. But if you think your daddy would mind . . ."

Thomas slid down, his shoulders touching the tree, and sat with his back against the trunk. Thomas knew his papa *would* mind. Macky's dad would mind, too.

"You'll get your britches wet sittin' in the snow," Macky said.

"What? Oh, my pants, you mean. I don't care about any *britches!*" Thomas said.

Mac Darrow crouched low with his hands folded between his knees. His gun was cradled against his chest. "What you so mad about?" he said.

It was true, Thomas was angry. He didn't know how to put it into words. "I'm not mad at you," he said at last.

"At my brothers, though." Macky studied his hands.

"I didn't say that," Thomas said. "But they weren't too nice, you know. Sneaking around, messin' up our kitchen . . ." He remembered it as if it happened yesterday. Food spilled everywhere, spoiling milk. Macky's big, dumb brothers, entering the house and doing damage. At last he and Macky were talking about it.

Macky nodded, as Thomas listed the devilment the Darrow men had done.

". . . sneaking in the house at night through the hidden passage and slapping those triangles on the walls."

Mac Darrow stared. "What?" he said.

"You know," Thomas said, "those triangles, like the ones the slaves used to find their direction north.

Really a cross reading. Only we found the ones your brothers made and put there, trying to scare somebody. And they're grown men, too. But we got them back for it."

Macky studied Thomas for a long time. One minute he looked as if he wanted to apologize for his brothers. The next minute he seemed astonished about something; then, confused. He looked and stared so long Thomas began to get a notion about something. But then he was reminded of something else he wanted to talk about. "Guess what?" he said, "My great-grandmother is coming to live with us. She's almost ninety." It sounded friendly, to say that.

Macky must have thought so, too, for he nodded, interested. He got up, saying, "You mind if I come over there? We can follow trails of beasts from over there just as easy."

"Why do you call them beasts?" Thomas asked as Macky came over.

"Mama calls them beasts. You never met my mama."

"No. I don't think I've seen her, either, all these months. Have I?" Thomas said. "At church?" It seemed odd now that he hadn't met her.

"Nope. She's an invalid," Macky said. "She stays in bed mostly."

Thomas tried not to look surprised. He'd never heard of anyone's mother being an invalid. Maybe if Macky's mother was eighty years old, she might be one.

He would've liked to have talked about it right then, but Macky went on.

"My mama likes to tell old-timey stuff," he said.

"Really?" Thomas said.

"Yeah. Not much else to do when you are lyin' down, being sick, then gettin' well over and over." He sighed. "King beast of the woods is one she tells."

"One what?" Thomas said.

Macky gazed at him. Serious and burly he was among the trees. He had a smooth, expressionless face. "Just about who in the woods is smartest. It changes," he said.

"I've never heard about anything like that before," Thomas said.

"It's old-timey stuff," Macky repeated. "Mama says, in olden times there was an Indian maiden girl always used to run through here. She had long black braids and a dress made out of buckskin, too."

Macky crouched down again, a little away from Thomas. He still may have been on Darrow land. But an invisible line was hard to read. Thomas was uneasy without a gun when a Darrow had one.

"Really?" Thomas heard himself saying. "An Indian girl?"

"Well, it's what Mama says," Macky said. Then, slyly, he grinned at Thomas. "And the story goes, not one man Indian could catch her. She'd come upon you in here, and like a breeze, she'd blow on by. Time you try to overtake her, she'd be so far ahead couldn't nobody catch her."

"She had a head start then," Thomas said.

Macky pursed his lips. "A young Indian man hid around, watching for her. He saw her and started to race her," he said. "She looked at him once, and he couldn't catch her. Others tried, but none ever could catch her."

"Why couldn't they?" Thomas asked, getting into the story. "An Indian man was used to running, I bet, and could outrun any woman."

"You think so? Well, she wasn't *any* woman. Turns out she was a ghost."

Thomas caught his breath. The slow grin spreading across Macky's face didn't register. A ghost! he thought. Slave ghosts were said to haunt the "crow" house of Dies Drear, but he'd never seen one. Old Pluto said he had, though. Said he'd even seen Mr. Dies Drear himself. Thomas noticed the silence then. He shivered all at once. "That's a ghost story," he managed to say.

"Well, might could be it is," Macky said mockingly. "It's what Mama told me."

"Is an invalid someone who is sick all the time?" Thomas asked. He was asking before he knew he would.

"My mama's not sick so much," Macky said. "Mainly it's how she acts sometimes." He seemed to ponder this. "She gets out of bed once in a great while, but we never know when."

"You mean, she won't get up every day?" Thomas said.

"Maybe two, three times a year," Mac Darrow said. "'Casionally every two months or so."

"Well, that's really too bad," Thomas said. He wasn't sure what to believe.

"Oh, we don't mind it much," Macky said. "Me and Pesty walk Mama down along the highway when she gets up. She likes that."

"That's right, she took Pesty in. . . . How could your mother take care of a baby if she was an invalid?"

Mac Darrow smirked. "She's not invalid all the time. Just sometimes when she lies down for six months."

"Well, I never heard of anything like that," Thomas said. "Pesty never once mentioned it." It finally came to him that Macky might be putting him on just to be important. "Maybe your mother's not any invalid," Thomas said.

Grinning, Macky got to his feet. He seemed to Thomas to tower above him. The grin never touched his large gray eyes flecked with yellow. "You callin' me a liar?" he said softly. "My mama is too an invalid. But there—look behind you! There's the Indian girl running!"

Thomas whirled around. "Ahhhh!" escaped him. He held on to the maple, terrified. The fog was rising. Snow, falling. How did it happen that the woods was pale with failing light, gloaming light? Dusk. The fog was ghostly white now. It danced and swayed. He almost thought he saw . . .

Ohhhh!

He looked to Macky for safety and found only the stillness and mist. He heard laughter—"Ha-ha!"—a ways off. Trees dripped, snow fell lightly where Mac Darrow had been. Only Macky's empty tracks were left.

Where . . . Macky!

But Mac Darrow had vanished. Thomas scrambled away from the great maple. He tore through the woods. He half believed the Indian maiden was somewhere near. He knew that Macky had been playing with him, but still, his fear rose on the twilight. He almost got turned around. Almost lost his way. They say ghosts walk at dusk. Run!

The crest of the hill had to be right before him. Was it? And the house, just down the hillside. Was it still?

His breath was ragged. He thought surely something was running after him, breathing down his neck. Oh no!

Thomas slipped and fell hard, as his feet slid from under him. He got up painfully on his knees and began crawling like a baby. His hands were fistfuls of snow. In another instant he was on his feet, running. And then he knew. Knew she—it—was there. Reaching, her dead-cold hand about to touch his shoulder. She would grab him and he would have to run until he would never run again. Ghosts were like that. Ghosts were . . .

He couldn't stand not knowing. He whirled around. His feet slid, but he kept his balance. There. Just as calm and cool as you please.

It was no Indian maiden. Macky had returned. He had been far enough behind Thomas that when Thomas spun around, there was room for Macky to step aside so they wouldn't collide.

The sound of Thomas's ragged breath filled the woods. No, he was out of the woods. He was on the edge of it, over the crest of the hill. His chest was heaving. I'm so dumb! he was thinking. He saw the house down there. Turned warily back to Macky.

Tall Mac Darrow was so still and remote against the trees. In the gloaming he gathered what light there was around him. He was ten feet away, standing with his hands poised on the gun. He cocked his head. "Seen my first rabbit of the day," he said. "Poor scared rabbit. You run that way, anything'll catch you."

"You tricked me!" Thomas managed to whisper.

Macky almost smiled. Just a faint twitching of his mouth as he looked off into the dusk. "You can come over my house anytime you want. I bet you too scared, though." He glanced once more at Thomas, at his defeat.

Thomas coughed suddenly. He bent double over a painful stitch in his side.

"There was, too, an Indian girl here. Once," Macky

said. Then he turned and walked away through the trees, east.

The hillside below Thomas gathered darkness. The lights went on in the Drear house. He walked down, feeling tired and sick of himself. I acted like a scared rabbit. Scared of a dumb story, he thought. We were just talking together. He was only putting me on. We could've hunted trails together! He asked me to come over there, and I had to go and say no. Why did I have to do that? But then he said I could come over anytime.

Maybe his mama is an invalid. Was it that I said she wasn't? Maybe he just wanted to get even with me for all of us scaring his brothers and his dad.

Friend or foe? I don't think we'll ever be friends!

At the backyard Thomas calmed down. He stepped up onto the veranda. The back door was right there. Safety, just in time. For it was night. He felt something rush behind him. Something ghostly blew out of the woods, swept down the hillside to climb the shadowy house of Dies Eddington Drear. Thomas slammed the door in the face of the chill wind before it could catch him.

3

Macky was a huge bear that came straight at him, lumbering right over him like a grizzly over a log. Thomas fell flat on his back as Macky's bear-clawed feet stepped on him.

It was a fleeting dream. Thomas awoke, feeling angry. He was lying facedown, with his nose pressed into the pillow.

What . . . time? he wondered. Oh. Dawn. He saw

faint light at the windows. It took him a moment to realize where he was, what day it was.

The easy chair was placed so he wouldn't have to wake up and see the black opening of the narrow fireplace. He stared at the floor-to-ceiling windows, which were bigger and longer than they needed to be. There's nothing out there, he thought. Just the day coming.

It's a school day coming. Which day? Oh, my brain is fuzzy!

He thought of yesterday. Pesty. Macky, at dusk. He closed his eyes. It's Friday, and I won't have to go to school. We're going to get Great-grandmother—what time? Must not be time because Mama would be here if it was, to make sure I'm up.

He closed his eyes, resting. But he couldn't help thinking about Macky and what had happened in the woods.

Glad it's light, he thought. Things look different in the light.

It was daylight when his mama came to wake him at six-thirty.

"Thomas. Thomas," she called softly.

He didn't open his eyes. He turned his head slightly, so he could put his chin in her palm, as her fingers gently touched his face.

"Come on," she told him. "You've got a long way, you and your papa."

They left at seven-thirty, after having dragged themselves out of warm beds, washed, dressed, and eaten. They would travel the distance in the family sedan, with the neat red trailer attached for Great-grandmother Jeffers's belongings. They never disturbed the twins, Thomas's baby brothers. The twins would sleep on until about eight. They would have two identical fits if they were to see Thomas and their papa going for a ride in the car without them.

"You take care now," Mr. Small said to Thomas's mama when they were ready to go.

"Mr. Pluto and I may do some house painting today," she told them. "I am interested in having my kitchen a little brighter."

"Be careful using the ladder," Mr. Small said.

"I'll be careful. Don't worry."

"Good," Mr. Small said.

"You should wait until I get back so I can help," Thomas told his mama.

"There'll be plenty paint left for you," she told him. "Plenty more rooms."

They left the house of Dies Drear behind. Martha Small waved goodbye from the front veranda. Thomas looked back, waving. Even in the growing morning the Drear house appeared dark and shadowy.

His mama grew smaller. She still waved. Thomas

had many impressions. His mama diminishing to doll size as the car sped away. So long, Mama.

The house got smaller, changed to a weathered doll's mansion from the giant crow house. Goodbye, *dreary* house. I'm glad to be gone from you today!

The gravel drive wound down and away from the hill. They crossed the old covered bridge and the stream that was so like a moat protecting the house. There was the woods at the top of the hill. Winter trees wore stripes of snow on their trunks and limbs. Zebras, Thomas thought. Winter wild animals.

He wondered if Mac Darrow was up yet, out tracking somewhere among those striped tree animals. Sighing, Thomas sat up straight beside his father as they headed south on the highway, out of town.

It was a long drive, but they would be able to get back home by eight or nine in the evening. Wouldn't do to stay overnight and leave his mama and his brothers home by themselves.

Anything might happen, Thomas thought. But we scared the Darrows away months ago, and nothing's happened since. It's a feeling, though. Papa feels it, too. But it's been a long while without any trouble. The Darrows stay there on their own farmland most of the time. If you didn't come into town on market or street fair day or go to church once in a while, you never would see them. Well, now there's Macky at school, in the woods.

But there's something about the house of Dies
Drear, too, Thomas thought. Like, maybe it's waiting.
Like, the time is up. The truce is over.

He shivered. That's too dumb, he told himself.

"Well, we're off," his father said, rousing Thomas
from his reverie.

"Good and off," Thomas said and his father
chuckled.

The heater was on. They were dressed in boots and
warm jackets, ready for anything. Ready for winter
highways and cold mountain highs.

"Can't wait to see Great-grandmother Jeffers,"
Thomas said. "It's been so long."

"Too long," his father agreed.

Great-grandmother Jeffers was his papa's grandmother. She was the only elderly relative that his father
had in North Carolina. Great-grandfather Canada
Jeffers had passed away some time ago.

Thomas patted his papa's shoulder and smiled up at
him. Mr. Small grinned, not taking his eyes from the
road.

They went south, first to Chillicothe, Ohio, and then
on to Portsmouth, where they picked up Highway 52.
The high hills made Thomas eager to see the mountains of North Carolina.

Thomas often made figures out of wood, and before
leaving home, he had begun a carving. Now he took
out the square piece of white pine he was working on

and his sharpened pocketknife. Whittling would give him something to do with his hands on the long drive.

His hands moved expertly over the wood. His left hand appeared to feel out the shape he wanted from the pine while the right hand carved it.

Mr. Small glanced around, amazed again at how his son seemed to be working with something soft, like clay. He could shave the wood so quickly.

"Wish I could stop awhile and watch you do that," he said admiringly.

"It's not going to be a whole lot," Thomas said.

"No? What is it to be?" asked his father.

"I'm not sure yet," Thomas said. Usually he didn't think about what he was whittling. "But there're some things on my mind."

He pictured his mama and his brothers back at the house of Dies Drear. He imagined the Drear house drawing away from the snow-white countryside. He thought about the old abolitionist Dies Drear, who had come from the East to help escaping slaves up from the Ohio River. Drear, moving through the house and outside it. Just vague notions and parts he recalled from the written history the foundation owners had given them about the Drear house and property, the section about the house as a station on the Underground Railroad.

Thomas's hands never stopped moving over the carving.

They stopped for lunch and to fill the tank with gas. They took the interstate down through Virginia. Near Fancy Gap they picked up the scenic Blue Ridge Parkway, which ran along the top of the mountains. Misty light and shrouds of rain hung over deep valleys. White patches of snow on the ancient range were swirled by fugitive winds. Thomas stared out the window, his hands turning and feeling the shape he was making in the white pine.

"Hope we get there soon. Hope the sun comes out." He spoke tiredly, suddenly bored with the long drive, of thinking about things over and over again.

The sun did come out in long shafts of sunlight, illuminating the western Appalachians.

"Nothing like my mountains!" he said, laughing.

"Not quite your mountains, but almost," his papa told him.

"When do we get to North Carolina?"

"Soon," his papa said. And it wasn't long after that that they crossed the state line. They headed southwest on the Blue Ridge Parkway, passing along between Sparta and Roaring Gap.

"Just another eighty miles or so," his papa said. Not long, and they were entering the Blue Ridge Mountains, the Pisgah National Forest.

The very space, the air, somehow shaped by the bluish distance, was different from anything farther north or anything Thomas had ever known. The mountains took his breath away.

In no time they found the little valley nestled where it had always been. And Great-grandmother Rhetty Jeffers's house the way it always was.

Wasn't a *house*, like houses in Ohio. It was a mountain cabin, really, planted in the valley. The cabin was smack against a hill that rose to mountains. Great-grandmother called all of the Blue Ridge "my *hills*." That way she made them fit her, made them her size so she could live with them, and they, with her.

They crossed a creek and wound down a lane that ended in front of the cabin.

There she was, standing by the lane, waiting for them: Great-grandmother Rhetty Laleete Jeffers.

4

She was dwarfed by the cabin and the hill rising behind it. Great-grandmother Jeffers wasn't more than four feet seven inches tall. The whole world and Thomas were taller.

Great-grandmother held herself tall, shoulders high. Her face was awash with happiness. She peered at Thomas and his papa as though trying to see above a sunrise. Her hair was swept up in a ball at the top of her head. Thomas was shocked to see that it had turned almost completely white.

"I *knew* it was you!" she exclaimed to them. She came forward gingerly, as though she were walking a tightrope. She wore a new coat and a dark blue dress and shoes to match. Her small, neat hands were clasped before her. "Heard the car winding 'round the hills. Great goodness, knew it was you, too!"

"Grandmother Rhetty!" Mr. Small exclaimed. He was out of the car, coming around the front. He folded her close. She felt breakable. Her arms, so thin. "You look well," he said, gently patting her shoulder.

"Oh, I'm fine, 'cept for some slowness."

Thomas came forward. "Great-grandmother Jeffers, hi!" he said.

"Well, Thomas, you come back." He lowered his head to her shoulder as she folded him in. "Wasn't expecting *you*. Now, I remember, your mama say on the telephone you'd be coming, too." She kissed his cheek warmly. She hugged him tightly, then held him at arm's length a moment to look him over. "Getting to be a big old boy! Missed you!"

"Uh-huh, missed you, too, Great-grandmother," he said.

She looked far into his eyes. "So," she murmured, "that Dies house, is it? You all had yourselves a something! I had my chicory roasting, don't you know? It takes care."

She believed that chicory had the power to ward off calamity. It must've, too, Thomas decided. For almost everything had turned out all right in the North.

Great-grandmother's property came right up to the laneside. There sat her blue mailbox on its post as they turned in the yard. There wasn't a walkway, just three or four stepping-stones, placed at points where the ground became soft after a hard rain.

Thomas took note of it all. That faded blue of the mailbox. It reminded him of something—that old gate of hers he used to paint. It was nowhere to be seen. Must've fallen down. He breathed deeply of the fresh country air. "Oh, it smells so good out here!" he said.

Great-grandmother Jeffers smiled. The smile was sad somehow. Then Thomas understood. He bowed his head.

"Not easy at all, leaving all this," Great-grandmother Jeffers said softly.

"Will you see it again?" Thomas asked.

"Oh, I plan to see it again. I won't get rid of it."

"You didn't sell it?" he said.

"I would never sell land like this," she said.

"Well, that's good. I thought you had."

"She's rented it, Thomas," his papa said.

She took hold of Thomas's arm for support but stood her ground. She was not yet ready to give up the view. It was her pride and joy.

"And you never minded staying out here all by yourself?" Mr. Small was saying, marveling. He loved the mountains, but he had always been ready to leave them when he had to. College. Work. Advancement.

Great-grandmother pursed her lips and said, "You know, after supper, couple times a week, I walk on over there to the Beau Chesters, my old friends."

Thomas remembered them.

"Silva make a pie every so often, from apples she picks just in season and keeps in the cellar," Great-grandmother went on. "That pie's most still warm by the time I get there. We set down and have it. Then Beau and me, we walk to a mountain. Silva can't walk these days, but she don't mind we do. And we climb some of the mountain, me and Beau."

She nodded eagerly. "Me, holding Beau's arm, and not a word need be spoken between us. Two old folks! It won't even matter to us if we can't make it back one time. Because of what you can see after supper! What you can just see!"

That made Mr. Small laugh outright in amazement. Here was his grandmother, near ninety, and she still could climb a mountain in order to see the beauty around her. "Then you walk back here after that?" Mr. Small asked.

She shook her head. "Silva ride me back in the pickup. We go slow, and we talk. And the night is falling," Great-grandmother said. "Silva puttin' on the lights. I most wait for that part, coming back."

"When she puts on the headlights?" Thomas asked.

Great-grandmother Jeffers gave him a long look as

though there were but the two of them, the way they had been together months ago. "It's what gets caught in the headbeams," she said, spoken gently. "Ghosts rise at dusk."

"Grandmother," Mr. Small said.

"I—I know that," Thomas said. He realized he did believe that. The Indian maiden! He knew dusk to be a time of caution, when what was supernatural could enter the mind.

Mr. Small cleared his throat as if to change the subject. Not knowing what to say, he remained silent. They stood there, surveying the cabin and the hill that rose sharply behind it. Beyond the hill, mountain faces and folds stood out from the silence as bold as thunder.

Words couldn't describe mountains planted forever just there, Thomas thought. It came to him that mountains had a talent for size, hugeness, just as he did for whittling. He smiled, daring to compare himself to them. Mountains were carved out of nature, as he carved from what was natural. Not too different, that mountain and me, he thought.

Thomas realized he was holding something. It was the carving. He'd had it in his hand the whole time. It was finished, and he hadn't realized.

"Great-grandmother, here," he said, and gave it to her for a present.

"Well, I'll be!" she said, taking it. "Who is it? Mr. Dies Drear?"

"No, it's a boy like me," he said. "Name of M. C. Darrow, called Macky."

"M. C. Darrow. Macky," she said. "Well, I'll be. He's your friend?"

"He's . . . a big boy," Thomas said.

She turned the carving over in her hands, feeling it and smoothing her fingers along its facets. "Heard about Darrows from your mother," she said.

Thomas nodded. "They're the ones caused us trouble," he murmured.

Great-grandmother Jeffers and Thomas both stared at the carving as she turned it over and around. It was a perfect rendering of Macky's head in miniature. "It's a fine portrait, I can just tell," she told her great-grandson. "Thank you, Thomas. I will cherish it," she said. "And I want to meet this Macky and his family one time."

"You do?" Thomas said. He stared at her, an idea dawning.

"Of course, I do," she said.

"That might prove difficult," Mr. Small said.

Great-grandmother smiled sweetly. "And I want to hear all about everything on the way to the North."

She slid the carving into her coat pocket and put her arm around her great-grandson. "Let's go on inside now," she told him. "I got everything ready."

Inside, it was the same place of old. Thomas had played here, slept here, so many times. Things were pulled apart now, but the house was still what he remembered. Great-grandmother had a few boxes full of things. She had furniture, bedding, and her mattress all ready to go. She had her best clothes on hangers, lying on the settee. There were two suitcases and a lamp she couldn't part with. His papa started taking her brass bedstead apart. After that was done, they loaded everything in the U-haul.

Great-grandmother Jeffers would take all the items that were special to her, such as the framed photographs she had kept for more than half a century. And she took her senior's walker, as she called it, which was a three-sided lightweight aluminum support. She used it to lean on when she had to.

Thomas and his papa worked fast and hard, going in and out of the house, back and forth. It was a strenuous exercise. I'm not any little kid, not anymore, Thomas thought. It felt good to be big and strong.

Then, all at once, they were finished. Thomas brushed his hands off. "That's all," he said.

Great-grandmother Jeffers nodded. "That's all that I'm taking." she said.

"It about filled the U-haul up, too," Thomas said.

She crossed the room and opened the door. She stood there, waiting for Thomas and Mr. Small to go out of the house. She meant to close the door herself on all that had been. She stood there, so tiny in her old cabin. And yet she was made large by this last moment's recollection of a lifetime.

5

"See?" Thomas said, excitedly. "It just goes up and up. Very high up. Straight up." It was dark out by the time they got home. They'd had a long and pleasant ride. Thomas talked all the way, telling Great-grandmother everything.

She had fallen asleep once, just a light dozing. She didn't think she had missed much. Darrow people with river names. The mother, an invalid. She'd heard that much. She recognized no division among peoples; no

enemies. Problems were solved through clear under-
standing. This one felt one way; that one, another. It
was the way with folks. No need to take sides.

"Well, what do you think?" Thomas asked her.

"About what?" she said back, teasing him. She knew
what he meant. She chuckled and patted his knee. The
car headlights gave them a fine view as they climbed
the snow-covered driveway up to the house.

"Thomas, it's a grand old house," she said, finally, as
they took her by the arms and gently helped her from
the car.

Thomas grinned. "Wait until you see everything," he
told her, guiding her to the porch. "These veranda
steps have the tunnel to the kitchen under them."

"So these are the ones," she said, and watched her
feet as she climbed up.

The front door swung open. There stood Mrs. Small
and the twins.

Great-grandmother Jeffers hollered when she saw
her granddaughter-in-law. "Goodness! Goodness! Martha, it's been too long."

"Oh, Grandmother Rhetty!" Martha Small said.
They hugged and kissed, laughing and nearly crying.
Great-grandmother Jeffers patted her granddaughter-
in-law as she patted everyone whom she loved.

Billy and Buster peeked around Mrs. Small with sol-
emn eyes.

"Hello, babies!" Great-grandmother Jeffers exclaimed, bending low to hug the boys. "Which one is

which one?" she said, not expecting an answer. The twins backed away from her, and she followed, right into the large entranceway.

"Look at us, standing here with the door wide open," Martha Small said. "Brrr! It's turning cold."

"Turnin' cold," the boys said in unison.

Great-grandmother studied them, amused. "Do they do that?" she asked. "Say the same thing at the same time?"

"They do it a lot," Thomas said.

"Don't you remember your grandma?" Great-grandmother Jeffers said to the boys. "The piney woods and my cabin? Remember how you loved my cotton patch? Hmm? Boys will be boys!"

It was Billy who first grinned from ear to ear. "Boys be boys!" he and his brother said.

Great-grandmother Jeffers opened her pocketbook and rummaged around in it until she found the ball of cotton she had brought in a silk handkerchief. She carried it as a good-luck charm.

It was Buster who reached for it and crushed its softness against his cheek. His eyes lit up. Both boys giggled. Quickly they came into Great-grandmother Jeffers's outstretched arms. "Gray-grahma!" they exclaimed, snuggling in.

"Yes, indeedy," she said, "and big as life! You remember *me*."

They remembered.

It took time getting her coat off, getting her situated

in the parlor, getting her warmed up and relaxed after such a long, stiffening ride. Great-grandmother Jeffers smoothed her hair back and looked around the long room at the floor-to-ceiling windows. "Who's going to clean such windows? Is that why you wanted me here?" she said.

They all laughed at that.

After a while they went into the kitchen.

"I knew I smelled fresh paint," Thomas said. "Look at that!"

The kitchen was painted the warmest yellow. "Looks just like spring!" Great-grandmother Jeffers said, beaming.

"I did it," Martha Small said proudly. "Mr. Pluto mixed the paint for me and set up my ladder."

"Bet you could get a good hourly wage for work like this, if you wanted," Mr. Small said, joking.

"I bet I could, too." She joked back.

They eased in around the kitchen table as Thomas set it for the supper his mama had prepared. Mr. Small served their plates from the stove and counter. The twins had already eaten, Martha said. But they enjoyed being at the table, climbing down and playing around, accepting hugs from their great-grandmother.

It took time to eat, to sip tea, and there was pie for dessert.

Time to catch up and to hear about the things that could not be spoken of over the telephone. Great-grandmother propped her arm on the table, resting her chin in her palm. "I want to see you-know-what-it's-called," she said. She meant the cavern of treasure. "I want to see everything, but best not to speak about that." She looked all around. "Do the little fellows know about you-know-what-it's-called?" she asked.

The twins were at once alert, knowing they were being talked about. Walter Small shook his head. "That's another thing. They're growing the way kids do."

There was a pause. "We keep them here around the house," Martha said. "But they will get away from you. I'm going to find a play school for them."

"Not to change the subject," Great-grandmother said, "but which is the wall in this kitchen that rises?"

Walter Small got up from the table and went over to a cabinet across from them. Beneath the cabinet was a panel that housed the machinery for the moving wall. He fiddled with the controls, picked up an object from one of the cabinet drawers, and added it to the mechanism. At once the kitchen wall silently slid up. The twins held on to Great-grandmother Jeffers on either side. The three of them stared. Before them was the black, gaping tunnel opening that led around to the front steps. Thomas found himself clutching the table edge.

Great-grandmother Jeffers leaned forward. She found the opening quite extraordinary. A tunnel of ages, she thought. Used by slaves, fugitives.

The dank air at the tunnel entrance seemed unsettled. She held her head cocked to one side as though she were listening to something.

"What is it, Grandmother Rhetty?" softly asked Thomas's mama.

Great-grandmother Jeffers shook her head. "Must've been nothing," she said. "There's sure nothing there."

"I've never liked that escape route," Mrs. Small said. "Never liked a wall that could slide up and down." Lightly she touched each twin on the head. Just then Billy disengaged himself from Great-grandmother and walked over to the cabinet with the panel. He began to fiddle with it.

"Hey! Don't touch that, Billy," Walter Small said. "Now, you're not to touch this panel, you hear?"

Great dark eyes shifted from his father to his brother Buster. Buster left Great-grandmother's side and toddled over to Billy to put a comforting arm around his brother.

"Look at that," Great-grandmother said, chuckling. "They are as cute as they can be!"

"Oh, they're cute all right," Martha said. "Cute into everything."

"Well, you have me now. They won't get by me," said Great-grandmother. "It's something, though. Big rooms. Moving walls and steps . . . What else moves around here besides them and you folks?" She laughed.

"The mirror in the front hall has a tunnel behind it," Thomas said.

"Well, you know, I just barely noticed that mirror out the corner of my eye as we came in," Great-grand-mother said. "So, the kitchen, the steps, and that mirror as you come in," Great-grandmother said. "Any more secret—" She stopped herself, at once knowing that she should not have asked.

Martha cleared her throat while Walter busied himself at the counter with the panel. The wall came sliding down.

"Papa . . ." Thomas began to speak.

"Now, Thomas," Mrs. Small said.

"Papa? There are more secret places?"

"I talk too much," Great-grandmother murmured.

Mr. Small sighed. "I suppose there are more secret tunnels and things," he admitted. "I haven't had the time to go checking, what with my job at the college and inventorying the you-know-what. I never had the complete plans of this house. I don't know if a complete set of drawings exists."

"You mean, there are other ways in here we don't know about?" asked Thomas. "I thought you knew everything about this house." I thought you were taking care of things, was what he really was thinking.

"You never know everything about a house this old," his papa answered.

"How are we going to sleep at night—" Thomas broke off. He knew he would have a hard time sleeping from now on. "I don't see how we're going to live, with strangers wandering in and out of our house," he muttered. All at once he felt letdown, anxious.

"We'll just have to secure the periphery," his father said.

"What's that supposed to mean?" Thomas said glumly.

"Your papa means," Great-grandmother told him, "that if you take care of what is going on on the outside, you don't need worry about anything coming or going on on the inside."

"That's right," his papa said. "We took care of the Darrows. I don't think it's likely they'll bother us again."

Thomas stared at his father. Would the Darrows have learned their lesson? And would the great treasure-house stay secure? He wasn't at all sure.

Great-grandmother Jeffers yawned. "Ooh! Now I know it's not that late," she said, smiling all around.

"You must be tired," Martha said. "Here, let's get you settled in your room. I put you next to Thomas, a little farther down on the opposite side of the hall from Billy and Buster."

"Anyplace will do me just fine," Great-grandmother said. "Please, don't fuss about me. I don't want to cost anything extra."

They all went to her room with her, surrounding her going up the wide old staircase.

"A fine house," she murmured. She laughed her high, mountain laugh.

Thomas couldn't get over the sweet sound of it.

6

They say dark, ghosty things walk haunted houses. Deep in the night, when the weather falls, the creeps come out and walk about the old Drear house, so the townsfolk say. They are half joking, but the children are quick to believe. Yet this night the house was quiet within its hidden places. Martha and Walter, the twins never awoke. Thomas slept. In her sleep Great-grandmother Jeffers rubbed her hands together, smoothed them, pressed them, until a dull aching faded. She awoke long enough to think: Barometer going down, my arthritis. Snow is not finished yet.

Outside, the wind rose, building a blizzard from out of the darkness. It soon raged against the house. Drear house shuddered but stood its ground. The night was blinded snow-white. Animals dug deep for safety.

Blasting wind swept the fields clean. Snow drifted four feet high against fences and treelines. But this storm couldn't last. It came and went in an hour, a preview of the hard winter to come. The night settled down in a snow light, bright as day. Huge, silent flakes came down abundantly. The little animals sniffed the air and crept about.

Thomas had burrowed deep beneath his covers. He awoke the instant the blizzard hit. He felt the house tremble and lift itself. He listened as the harsh drone of the wind filled his brain. He got up to look out of the window, and he was still half asleep. The windows were frosted over. He could see little. The wind roar filled every space inside him. He got back in bed. The place he had been beneath his covers was still warm. He burrowed again, a little animal himself. He had no thought of tunnels, intruders, or sliding walls. He was gone to sleep. No specter, no shadow of stealth invaded the Drear house this night.

Nothing so certain could be said of the cave on the other side of the hill from the Drear house, where Mr. Pluto lived.

Pluto underground. It was a large cave, one wall of

which was false, but no one would ever guess that it was. Behind the false wall was the secret entryway down to the great cavern of treasure deep within the hillside.

Mr. Pluto had enjoyed the day, helping Mrs. Small with her kitchen painting. He went in and out of the house for her, fetching paint from the shed in a corner of the backyard—turpentine, paint thinner. Women always thought that paint came in small portions, a pint or two high, was his smug opinion. Women never saw a full can. His late wife never had. He had given her half a can of paint to work with long ago, the way he had done for Mrs. Small today. He enjoyed mixing the paint for the womenfolk.

And those little boy twins—they were two pistols! Calling him Mist Blue-doe, Mist Blue-doe, it sounded like. He had watched out for them while Mrs. Small carried on with her kitchen painting. He bundled them in their snowsuits and took them outside. Gave them brushes to paint the shed. He'd gone back to help Mrs. Small. And by the time he remembered to check on the boys, they had painted their snowsuits, their faces, and their hair. They had rolled in the yellow. Well, a good thing Mrs. Small used water-based paint. It wasn't hard to clean up the boys and launder their suits. And he'd gotten them all clean, all fixed up. Had their snowsuits washed and dried in the big new washer and dryer the Smalls had got. Mrs. Small said he could even bring his own clothes over for the washer. But he preferred the clothesline right inside his cave. His wife and he long ago had hung the clothes in the cave in winter.

And hurrying out to the shed some more for Mrs. Small. Mixing or pouring more paint. Dry walls do take the paint!

Later he sat down at the kitchen table and had soup with the boys. Mrs. Small stopped her work. "That's a good time to stop," she had said, "soup time." And she had heated up the homemade soup. She had given the bowls over to Buster to set up the table. And the whole time Billy watched, holding on to Mr. Pluto's knee. The first taste of the thick vegetable soup had made him shiver, it was so good.

It was a fine afternoon in the Drear house, Pluto thought on the way home. Halfway up to the hilltop, where there were woods, he thought to turn around.

He didn't know why he turned, but maybe he had heard something. And there were the little fellows— Buster, first, with Billy coming on fast behind him. They had sneaked out of the house, without one sweater on between them. They looked as full of mischief as when they had painted themselves.

His heart had gone cold. For behind the boys someone had been stalking, like some stealthy beast of prey. He'd almost seen who it was, too. Almost, but not quite. Well, he was not as quick as once. His eyesight was not as good. The little boys had no idea someone was there. By the time he'd turned, whoever it was was already gliding away off the path, fading away in the trees. Pluto stood his ground, listening to the air, it must've seemed to the little boys.

"What am I going to do with you boys?" he said finally, easily setting the pace back toward the house. They held on to his big, leathery hands.

Pluto took them clear back inside, into the kitchen. He knew the back door should stay locked. Neither he nor Martha Small had locked it. Mrs. Small had been upstairs but on her way down.

"Stay put a minute," he had warned the boys, "just until I get away from here, and I won't tell on you."

They understood. Billy and Buster had stood holding hands. He had spoken softly to them. "Now, don't you ever run off again, you hear? Or I'll have to tell your mama." And he left them there, hating to leave them, but he had his own business to attend to.

He had been halfway home the second time. At the top of the hill where the woods began, he thought about the someone who had been following. He'd eyed each side of the woods along his way but saw only trees. It wasn't the boys someone was stalking. Someone is spying on *me,* he'd told himself at the time. Waiting for him to let down his guard.

At eveningtime Little Miss Bee had come by to go into the great cavern with him. It was the name he had given Petsy Darrow. Long before the Small family moved here, he and the child had shared his secret. It was a dangerous business, keeping such great wealth. But Little Miss Bee was a child of trust. Trust the child never to be seen slipping away from home! He and she would sit down among the treasures like granddaughter and grandfather. And after, he would lead her most of the way home; she would slip inside the house again, unseen and unheard.

"Best we not visit at night," he told her lately, sensing something troubled, unsettled about her. "Best you stay close to home in the evenings, Miss Bee."

And she had said, "See you tomorrow then."

"Remember," he'd warned her as she left never to tell the secret.

"I always remember," she whispered, and left him.

Pluto underground in the blizzard night, dreaming his dream. It was not a nightmare. The dreaming did not terrify him after the first shock. Seeing the dead. Dreaming his dream of old. He did not wake from it in a cold sweat.

Dies Eddington Drear came to stand at the foot of his bed. He told Pluto whether he was close to finding the treasure.

But why keep dreaming this dream? Pluto would think when he awoke. I have found the treasure. Mr. Small, he taken care that the treasure is safe. But maybe it's not so safe. Something going on. Somebody got their eye on me. Following. Little Miss Bee, so unsettled.

His own cave where he lived. Why the cave, why live that way? the townsfolk asked, oh, years ago. And why not? he had replied. It was the old way, the way of fugitives, escaped from bondage.

Now the cave was as secure from weather as he and nature could make it. From within, the sound of the night's blizzard that had awakened Thomas was faint. No hint of any change to the falling, silent snow. Two great, thick wood plank doors secured the cave opening. A heavy bar locked it from inside.

There was a tunnelway that led from his cave to another chamber to an underground stable he had made into stalls. There his horses ate and slept in foul weather. In the cave proper there was a fire banked for the night in the fireplace. No red embers showed, but the gray-black coals still held heat. The heat took away what chill moisture crept in from outside.

Pluto lay on his bed asleep. He was a thin elderly man, straight and long, but somehow fragile beneath old Indian blankets. His eyes moved under their lids, and then they opened in a dream delirium. His arms lifted, pointing in front of him to the foot of the bed. Someone was there. He saw the abolitionist standing there. Drear's beard was as long and as white as Pluto's.

Dies Drear of the great eastern family of money. He had saved poor fugitives from certain recapture. He loved freedom. To Drear those who practiced slavery were heathens, doomed for eternity.

And dreaming, Pluto waved his arms and made his

point. He murmured, talking nonsense. He and Drear were arguing.

"I'm taking the treasure," Drear was saying.

"You can't take it, it's not yours to take!" Pluto shouted.

"It is mine, I brought it here. I saved it. I have someone to give it to."

"Who!" cried Pluto. He felt as if there were a fire within him. "Who are you giving it to? It belongs to slaves! You can't take my forge." He meant the treasure. He was dreaming of his forge, where he heated, hammered, and shaped iron, but it was the wealth of the cavern he had meant to say.

"I can and I will take it," Drear said. "But I forgot where I put it. Tell me where I put it, Mr. Pluto."

Pluto felt such fear and anguish. He squirmed, suddenly sick of the dream turned to nightmare. He tried to wake himself. He sat up, blinking, feeling as if his shoulders were bars of ice.

The figure at the foot of the bed was a solid form. Pluto couldn't be sure who or what it was.

He fell back. The dark at the foot of his bed hadn't moved. Pluto stared at it, panting. He felt chills shaking his body. A thin layer of sleep was ground fog on his brain. Slowly he sat up again. "Who?" he murmured. It hurt him to sit up and lie down so much. Hurt his back.

"It's Drear," the dark form said. "I misplaced it. Where did I put that treasure?"

Suspicion was like something Pluto could wrap around him. Like the great black cloak he wore to protect himself from old age. Somewhere deep down he knew he must avoid even dreaming anything that might give away the wealth that was hidden.

"I quit this dream," Pluto said out loud, dreaming. "Quit it!"

The form wouldn't go away. Its voice had reminded Pluto of someone, someplace. He had no idea what Drear's voice would be like. But dreaming, he knew that this voice was too ordinary to be the great man's.

"Huh? Wha—Huh?" Pluto said, rising out of bed.

The specter came around the bed, heading for the passage from the room on the side. It was almost there, but so was Pluto. Pluto leaped for it before he knew what he saw might be real. In dreams he did such things. In dreams he was always youthful and strong.

He and the form struggled. *Is this real? It can't be Dies Drear!* It was not as long and as tall as Pluto. What it wore was dark and soft, cool as night rain. It had more than enough strength to subdue two old men. Whirling, breaking away, it knocked Pluto to the cane floor. Pluto grabbed its foot. *Barefoot? No, slippery, rubbered foot, wet with icy cold. This can't be a dream!* It kicked out, caught Pluto under the chin. A perfect clip it gave old Pluto. Stunned, he thought he heard the thing sigh with despair at what it had done. He passed out.

Then it was dawn and gray cave light. Impossible to tell how the morning got into the cave. Pluto found himself on the floor. How'd I get here? he wondered. "Must've fallen out of bed," he said out loud. "Cold." His throat was sore and raspy. "Dreams." He knew he had dreamed. Drear had been in his dreaming. For the thought of the old abolitionist was still with him. What was it about this time? He could not clearly remember. What more else could it be about?

"Been dreamin' all night," he murmured. "I'm tired. Thought I got rid of all such dreams." Carefully he moved his legs and arms and moaned, got back into bed. He moved his jaw around, but it seemed to be in one piece. How did it get to be sore?

A cold shiver of fear climbed his back. He shook it off, shrugged it away. He would not allow himself even to think that anyone could invade his cave.

"I'm too old and tired." He sighed inwardly. Later he must take a tonic, get rid of a raspiness. He couldn't bring himself to get up yet, fix the fire, make his coffee. He was soon asleep again.

For a while he slept heavily. But then his throat seemed to thicken inside. It hurt him in his sleep, and he couldn't swallow well. All moisture appeared to leave his skin. A slight fever rose. So, again, did his dreaming.

7

Thomas's eyes sprang open. He was lying on his back as straight as a board. His room was bright with morning. Saturday. He got up and hurried to get dressed in his weekend outfit of corduroys, sweater, jacket, and hiking boots. No telling what he and Pesty would do today, but he had a good idea. That is, if she came over today.

She ran off from me, day before yesterday, he

thought. She had to know Macky was there in the woods, and she didn't tell me.

Still, he expected her today.

By seven-thirty Thomas was downstairs. His mother was up and about; he had heard her in the parlor and in the dining room. Now, she was in the kitchen. Much earlier he'd heard her leave and a car going down the drive.

Must've been Papa going. Mama driving him to work.

His papa had only two classes to teach on Saturdays. After that he would have time for lunch at home; his mama would pick him up in the car.

When he looked out the front door, Thomas saw Pesty just stepping up onto the veranda. He poked his head out, whispering, "Shhhh. Be a minute," and closed the door again.

Pesty stood there with her hands pressed against her mouth. Her alert eyes watched the closed front door. Thomas pulled on his gloves and went quietly out. He walked around her and down the steps. "Wait!" she said.

"Shhhh!"

She caught up with him. "Didn't your grandmom come visit?"

"I told you, she's not—she's my great-grandmother Rhetty Laleete Jeffers, and she's here. And this is where she'll live with us forever, too," Thomas said.

"When can I meet her?" Pesty asked.

"Not yet, she's not even up," Thomas said. He was heading toward the shed where the twins had played and painted. They went around behind where they were hidden from view. They leaned against the side. Pesty peered anxiously at Thomas.

"It snowed," he said by way of greeting.

"It blizzard, too," she said. "I heard it." She smiled brightly at him. But Thomas didn't feel much like smiling back. She could tell then that he was not happy with her.

"Escort service!" she said suddenly, mischief in her eyes.

"Shhh!" he said. "Girl, what's on your mind!"

She covered her mouth again a moment. She'd forgotten that the house was still half asleep. "I mean, I'll escort your great-grandmother to Mr. Pluto's."

"You mean, we," he said, but changed his mind. "Don't you think someone who lives hereabout should come to meet the new neighbor first?" Thomas didn't wait for an answer. "We'll go over and get him and bring him back here to meet Great-grandmother Jeffers," he said. "That's what we'll do. That's proper."

At once he set off, going around the hillside toward old Pluto's. Pesty followed, upset that she hadn't known what was proper. They would be the escort service for Mr. Pluto.

Snow packed beneath their feet. She had an idea of her own. "Mr. Thomas! You-all can come over to my house, too. Your grandmama can meet *my* mama!"

The idea stunned Thomas for a moment before he said, "Pesty, please don't call me mister." Maybe it would be all right to visit Mrs. Darrow.

"See, it's okay for my great-grandmother to come visit your mother," Thomas said. "See, because she, your mother, is—is an invalid."

Pesty looked down at her hands.

"Why didn't you ever tell me that?" Thomas said. He stopped to face Pesty. "You let Macky tell me when it's you and me together every Saturday, and then some. Macky says that your mother won't get up out of bed for months at a time."

Thomas left off when he saw how uncomfortable talk of her mother made Pesty. She had turned sadly away, and somewhat guiltily, too, it seemed to him.

"You could've told me your brother was out there the other day," he said, changing the subject. "You didn't have to run off like that."

Pesty clutched one hand in another and seemed about to cry.

They were friends, and he was quick to soothe her. "Do you feel okay? Did you have some breakfast?" he asked her.

She nodded. She was missing buttons from her coat, he noticed. She had no hat on, and her neck was bare. "Pesty, where are your mittens?"

"Somewhere, I don't know."

"Well. Here, take mine."

"No!" she said. "I don't care nothing about it. I'll put my hands in my pockets."

"Oh, girl! Well, come on then!" He sprang ahead of her to lead.

Cutting across the hill and around was not difficult. Most of the snow had been swept away by the blizzard. Snowdrifts were like white ocean waves among a stand of shade trees just above them. The white waves bulged, about to break over them.

"Look at them over there!" he said over his shoulder again.

"The drifts look deep," she answered.

"Maybe later we'll jump in them," he told her.

"They'll be over my head," she said.

"You won't drown," he told her.

"But how do you breathe under the snow?"

"There's air, you'll see," he said.

"You'll have ta go first," she said.

"Of course, I will," Thomas answered.

There was a clearing just before Mr. Pluto's cave. They never cut across the clearing. Thomas felt like a target when he was in the midst of it. He skirted the clearing to come upon the cave at the side.

The heavy doors of the cave entrance were closed tight. Gently Pesty knocked. There was no answer, so she knocked a little louder. Still no response. She placed the flat of her hand on each door. She pushed and pushed again. But the doors did not spring open as they usually did.

"He must got them barred from inside," Pesty said.

"Darn! I'd better call to him," Thomas said.

"Unh-unh, don't call him," Pesty said. "He must be sleeping; only it's too late for that." She looked puzzled.

"He might be in the great you-know of the you-know-what."

The way Thomas avoided saying the secret made her smile. "He always will wait for me," she said.

Thomas had an anxious moment at the same time Pesty did. They stared at each other. "He ain't ready to die," she said finally.

"What do you mean by 'ready'?" he said, astonished.

"They know things like that—old folks," she said.

That could be true, he thought, but he said no more about it. "We have to get in there, see if he's all right. Maybe I'd better go home, call my papa," Thomas said. "Papa could break in the doors."

"Nobody's gone break them old doors, not unless they got an ax," she said.

"Well, there's an ax at the house. Papa got it not long ago," Thomas said.

"Don't need an ax," she said, walking away from him.

"Hey!" Thomas watched her go a second before he followed. "Where are you going to, Pesty? You intend to disappear the way you did the other day?"

Pesty lowered her head, looking ashamed. Then she went on around to the right, away from the cave doors.

The ground angled down in front where the doors were, for here was a fault to the land. Long ago the ground had faulted on the outside top of the cave, above the doors. That was the reason anyone coming up to the cave doors stood before them on lower ground.

On the right and to the rear fault the top of the cave slanted down, like a thatch-covered roof. Pesty stood there at the downward slant. She reached for a clump of frozen thatch and held it tightly in both hands.

"Pesty, what do you think you are doing?" Thomas asked, coming up to her.

"Pulling," she said. She looked all around; then she gave the thatch a hard yank. A chunk of it came off like the lid to a barrel. Not only did the thatch come off, but a jagged, crooked circle of ground came with it.

Thomas gaped. For there was a black hole in the slanted ground. Pesty quickly climbed up toward the hole.

"Pesty!"

"Shut up, Mr. Thomas," Pesty said. "You want somebody . . ." But the rest of her warning was lost as she slithered into the black opening.

8

Oh man! Another tunnel? A secret way into Pluto's cave, Thomas thought. I never knew! Papa never knew. Or Mr. Pluto either?

He climbed up, going in just the way Pesty had, before he knew he would. I'm not going to like this, he was thinking. The way was narrow and black. He slithered in blindly and breathed the dank odor of a closed underground. There was no way to turn around to find out if he could see the light from the thatch opening.

Too narrow to turn, he thought. If you try it, you might get stuck. Oh don't panic. "Pesty!"

"You got to move on down some," he heard Pesty say. He was so relieved that she was there. "I'm right by you," she said. "Just move on."

"But how?"

"Move on! I got to git back there and grab that hole cover."

He moved forward, sensing Pesty going by him. There must have been a niche in the tunnel side for her to fit into. Suddenly he remembered he had seen something attached to the cave lid. Rope and chain, twisted together. Must have been staked inside the cave wall somewhere, so the cover wouldn't roll away. Someone in the tunnel would be able to pull it up by the rope chain and close up the hole as though it had never been. Pesty was about to do that.

Take it easy, he thought. Slaves must've been scared sometimes. Did they ever use this tunnel? It's so dead dark.

He wasn't going to move very far; he didn't want to bump into anything unexpected. Then she was there behind him. "Move on out, Mr. Thomas," she told him. "It ain't far now."

He never thought to correct her about saying "Mr. Thomas." "Me, go first?" he said.

"I can't get by you here. You got to go on first," she said.

He knew he had to move. And he was moving, crawling and scooting along; crouching, never able to stand upright.

"Pesty! Where are we—" The tunnel turned abruptly. Thomas found himself up against the cave. "It ended," he said. "We have to go back."

"You just push at the wall with your hands," Pesty said. "Press your hands, and slide them over on the right."

Thomas put his hands against the coolness of the cave barrier in front of him. It was covered with moss. Damp rock and dirt. Gingerly he touched it, placing his palms against it. He pushed, pressing to the right as he did so.

It felt as if a boulder were rolling away, sliding out from under his palms. "I don't believe this! Is this tunnel a real old one?" he asked.

He saw light, like shade. He saw huge horses right there in front of him.

"Just move real slow, Mr. Thomas. They ain't going to bother you," Pesty said.

As if in a trance, Thomas moved out of the opening and into the place of horses. It was a large horse stall. The horses whinnied softly and made room for him.

Pesty stepped out then. She went to the animals to pat their noses and stroke their necks. Their heads bobbed up and down as she slid her hands along their manes. They nuzzled her. "Good horses!" she told them. "Good ol' Sam and Josie. You Mr. Pluto's buggy ride. Haven't been let out.

"They should be outside by now," she told Thomas. "I'll have to take them later."

She left the horses. Thomas followed, closing the stall behind him.

"That back there is a secret tunnel," he said to her.

"Might be secret to you, not to me," she said.

"You never told us about it," Thomas said.

"Nobody never did ask me. Wouldn't want it to get known."

He was dazed by what had happened, and he couldn't think of anything to say. He followed her, realizing they were in familiar territory.

They walked inside Pluto's cave. And there was Pluto, sitting by the fire, sipping from a glass carafe. He had a piece of wool wrapped around his throat.

Just like that, Thomas thought. A secret way in to see Mr. Pluto. He was amazed that ordinary life went on while he'd done something so strange.

There was the smell of camphor in the cave. Pluto looked surprised when he first saw them; then he smiled. "I see you come the back way. Well, I heard somebody at the door. Couldn't yell. Hoarse. Figured whoever it was would come back later." He raised the steaming carafe in greeting. "This here potion is for a slight cold in my throat."

"Is it tea? Can I have some?" Pesty asked. "Does it taste good?"

"Tastes pretty bad, don't think you'd like it, Little Miss Bee," Mr. Pluto said. "But it sure has helped me some this morning fit for a fright."

"You feelin' sick?" Pesty asked him. She put her arm around his shoulder.

"It's nothing much, some raspiness," he said. "But, Miss Bee, I feel almost well when I see your face." His mood changed, and his brows knitted together. "I won't be scared. Whoever it was," he muttered to himself, "he won't be gettin' nothing out of *me*."

"Wha—what?" Thomas said, not sure he had heard right.

But Pesty was saying, "Mr. Pluto, you think you are well enough to meet Mr. Thomas's great-grandmama?"

"Oh my!" Mr. Pluto exclaimed. "That's right! I been feelin' out of sorts some, I forgot she was coming. But you give me a day and I'll be over there to welcome your great-grandmama, Thomas."

"You can't come back with us today?" Pesty said.

"Miss Bee, I get my feet wet again and I'll have the pneumonia."

"It's okay," Thomas was quick to tell him. "It can wait until tomorrow or the next day. Anyway, Great-grandmother Jeffers is going to stay with us forever."

"That's plenty time for me and her to get acquainted," Pluto said, smiling at them.

Thomas was pensive before he said, "Did you say

someone wasn't getting anything out of you? Mr. Pluto
. . . was there somebody here?"

"Dreams, is all, I expect," Pluto said. He didn't want
to upset Thomas, or Pesty either. "But I feel a chill
wind. Yes, it is," he thought to add. "I do like to stay
close to home such times."

He turned his attention to Pesty. "Miss Bee, can you
take care of the horses?"

"Sure can," she said. "Mr. Thomas and me will do
them."

Thomas nodded to show that he was willing.

"Well, then I'm going to putter around here," Pluto
said. "Then I'll lay down awhile again. That's what old
folks have to do when they get soreness. They have to
lay down awhile again and again." He chuckled.

"We could call a doctor for you," Thomas said.

"No, son, you wait until I kick the bucket before you
call the doctor."

"Mama calls the doctor sometimes when I or my
brothers are sick," Thomas said.

But Mr. Pluto waved his hand, wouldn't hear of it.
"After the horses you-all can go on back home. I'm just
going to lie about most the day. Keep warm."

"You mean we won't . . ." Pesty began.

Mr. Pluto stopped her before she finished.
". . . won't go there this day." He cocked his head
slightly toward the hidden entrance to the great cavern. "Maybe walls have ears," he added. "Real folks,
maybe, living in dreams."

Pesty looked solemnly at him.

"Miss Bee," he said, "see how the snow lay. See to the *way* east and west."

Pesty was going out, headed for the horses. Thomas followed, wondering what Pluto had meant. See to what way?

They went from the cave room down the short, dim tunnel back to the double stall where Pluto kept his horses. The horses neighed, glad to see Pesty again. Thomas saw that the cave wall at the back of their stall was closed. He hadn't noticed when Pesty did that.

Nobody would ever know, he thought. But somebody knew. Pesty knew.

The horses, Sam and Josie, were bridle- and harness-wise. And it was easy to slip short ropes around their necks to lead them from the double stall.

Thomas and Pesty brought the horses back up the tunnel into the cave. Thomas unbarred the plank doors. Mr. Pluto was there, with a woolen throw about his shoulders, still sipping his tonic.

"Bye then!" Pesty called to him. "See you tomorrow!"

"Bye!" Thomas said.

They headed the horses around to the fenced meadow. They cleared off the snow in the water trough and broke through the thin ice. There was still fresh water beneath. They added to it with snow that melted at once. Then they saw to the oats and hay.

"We still have most of the morning to fill up," Thomas told her after they finished.

Pesty stared around them. She commenced walking the hillside from east to west. It was in the east that she bent low to study the snow-covered ground.

"What are you doing, girl?" Thomas said.

"Wait a minute, Mr. Thomas," she said. She scraped away a top layer of snow. The ground did look slightly different here.

"Snow melted sometime in the night," she told him. "Air turned warmer."

"You see all that by just looking at the snow?" he asked. He hunkered down beside her.

"Well, now it's colder," she said. "The snow is packed and frozen and one layer stuck over the next, see?" she said.

If there had been tracks, they were certainly hidden now. But she knew something. She straightened up, gazing off to the west. She thought she saw impressions at intervals in the snow, going off into the woods.

She shivered slightly. Pesty could stand the cold most of the time. She had seen and walked snows and snows. There wasn't much else to see in the wintertime. She knew tracks—melting, frozen, slippery, animal, human. "No kind I ain't seen," she murmured to herself, "but are these tracks?"

"That's what you are searching for—tracks?" Thomas said softly, matching the level of her voice. He looked. Pretty soon he knew there had to be something there through the snow. The trail was nearly invisible. But someone had been where they were, maybe had come the way they had, through the hole, and had gone off the same way. It could have happened sometime in the night. "Yes, but whose tracks?" he said finally. "Was it—was it one of your brothers?"

When she was silent, he said, "Pesty, who was it came here? Did he come into the cave the way we did?"

"*He?*" she said. "I don't know no *he.*"

"You know something. Now tell me!"

"What you talking about, Mr. Thomas? There was nothing. Those tracks is just animals going and coming, hunting shelter."

She was protecting someone. Thomas was sure of it. "Was it Macky?" he said.

But she went on as if she hadn't heard the question. "I come from here last night myself," she said, "after evening, to see Mr. Pluto, and it was snowing.

"Is it time to meet your great-grandmama?" she said sweetly. She did not look him in the eye. "Can I meet her now?"

"Yeah!" Thomas said. "That's a good idea. She'll be up by now."

"So . . ." Pesty said.

"Let's go!" they said together.

They left then. Thomas let mysterious snow tracks drift out of his mind. Never seems to take as long going back home, he thought. Wonder why?

9

Great-grandmother Jeffers awoke to a pleasant day. The next moment she had to be seeing double. Leaning over her were two identical faces. The twins were dressed up, their hair combed, and they were grinning at her exactly the same way.

"Gray-grahma," they piped in unison.

"Well, good morning!" Great-grandmother Rhetty Jeffers said.

"Good mornin'," said Billy Small. At least Great-grandmother Jeffers thought it was Billy.

Buster jumped on the bed and crawled up beside her. He thrust a picture book at her. He had been holding it all the while.

"Read it me," Billy said, climbing up on the bed and squeezing in next to his brother. Buster nodded.

Delighted, Great-grandmother Jeffers sat up comfortably against her pillows. "Let's just see what it is you've got," she said.

"Free Bears," Billy said.

"The Three Bears!" Great-grandmother said, taking the book from Buster. "How long has it been since I laid eyes on *The Three Bears*! My! Used to read *The Three Bears* to Thomas all the time. And something called . . ."

"Hector Protector," Thomas said. He was there, standing in the doorway, with Pesty Darrow peeking around behind him.

"Well, good morning, Thomas," Great-grandmother Jeffers said. "And good morning, there," she added to Pesty.

"Hi! This is my friend," Thomas said, coming in with Pesty. "She's Pesty Darrow, the sister of Macky. I told you about him."

"Well, I'm pleased to meet you, Miss Pesty," Great-grandmother said.

"This is my great-grandmother Jeffers," Thomas said to Pesty.

Pesty grinned and nodded. "Good morning," she said.

"Good morin, Pesty!" piped Buster.

"Good *mornin'*, *Pesty*," Billy said, correcting him.

"Hi, y'all," Pesty said to the boys.

Great-grandmother grinned at Pesty. "Just call me Grandmother Rhetty if you want to," she told her. Then she turned to Thomas and said, "Yes, it was *Hector Protector*. I remember now.

"Thomas, you still have that book?" asked Great-grandmother.

"I think so. I must've brought it."

"Well, I hope so," she said. "I'd like to read them old *Hector Protector*."

"Hec, Brec," said Billy.

Buster regarded him for a moment and then grabbed him. And they both fell over on the bed, giggling.

"You guys stop it!" Thomas said. "You're going to hurt Great-grandmother, roughhousing like that."

"They love to roughhouse," Pesty told Great-grandmother.

"Billy and Buster might muss up their pretty outfits," said Great-grandmother. "Where are they going, all spiffied up this morning?"

"Mama said something about taking them into town to look around at the nursery schools," Thomas said.

"Oh, that's right," Great-grandmother said. "But I didn't know she was planning on it today."

"Guess she knew we would keep you busy, me and Pesty," Thomas said.

"Well," Great-grandmother said.

"Great-grandmother," he went on, "we've been over to Mr. Pluto's already."

"That so?" she said.

"Yeah, and Mr. Pluto can't come over until tomorrow. He's got a sore throat, but he's not real sick," Thomas said.

"Well, I'll bring him some of your mama's soup, how's that?"

"Or one of her pies," Thomas said eagerly.

"I'd better get up from here then," Great-grandmother Jeffers said. "I slept so good!"

"There was lots of noise last night," Thomas said. He knew he must go on talking to keep her in bed a little longer. His mama had a surprise.

"Noise," the boys said to Great-grandmother.

"It sounded like a blizzard came real fast," Thomas said.

"A blizzard!" Great-grandmother said. "I didn't hear a thing."

"Well, I did. I think I heard it," Thomas said.

"Goodness, what's this congregation?" Mrs. Small came in, ready for a morning in town. "Morning, everybody," she said, eyeing Thomas, Pesty, and the boys. "Grandmother Rhetty, good morning!" Martha Small said. "I hope you slept well, even with the storm last night."

"Good morning to you," Great-grandmother said. "Oh, I did sure sleep, I sure did. Martha, darlin', this is the best old house for sleeping."

"Don't I know it," Martha said. "But I hope some little boys and a big boy and girl didn't burst in here to wake you up."

"Pesty and me have already been outside," Thomas said.

"Pesty and I," Mrs. Small corrected.

"Well, Billy and Buster were crawling all over Great-grandmother when we got here," Thomas said.

Billy and Buster scrunched low against Great-grandmother Jeffers. They grabbed the blanket to cover their faces. Buster thought to put *The Three Bears* on the very top of his curly head.

"Don't think that's going to hide you two," said Mrs. Small.

"Don't scold them, Martha. I just hope they come in to greet me every morning like this," Great-grandmother Jeffers said. "I love to see their faces exactly alike smiling at me. And we're going to read a story."

"You'll get to hear a story later, boys," Martha Small told her sons. At once she put a finger to her lips, warning them to keep still. They were quick to understand. They watched her as she winked at Thomas. Thomas hurried out. They could hear him taking the stairs two at a time.

"What are you-all up to?" Great-grandmother Jeffers said, smiling.

"Read me!" Billy commanded. Buster was searching for the book. He'd lost it in the jumble of bedcovers. Billy gave him a push.

"Stop that," Martha told him. "There'll be time for stories later. Grandmother Rhetty, I'm sorry, but we have to be going. Boys, we have to go visit some schools. They are getting to be too much even for me," Mrs. Small explained.

"But the both of us together, couldn't we both handle them?" Great-grandmother Jeffers asked.

Mrs. Small shook her head. The land, full of caves, was on her mind. It was no place for boys to be free to roam. "It's time they played with other children. You know, they never have much," she said.

"Billy, Buster, move out the way!" Thomas yelled. He was back. Pesty had slipped out of the room, unnoticed, and now had returned with him. He had a breakfast tray for Great-grandmother Jeffers. It was the surprise.

"Oh!" Great-grandmother exclaimed.

"I thought it would be nice if we spoiled you today," Martha said.

"Oh my! You-all shouldn't've gone to such trouble," Great-grandmother said.

Gingerly Thomas carried the tray to her bedside. He was perspiring, for it hadn't been easy getting up the stairs.

The twins scrambled to the foot of the bed as Thomas and Pesty placed the tray across Great-grandmother's lap. The tray had panel legs that rested on each side of her. "Look at this!" said Great-grandmother Jeffers. "Thomas, you made these pancakes?"

"No, I just took the plate out of the oven and put everything on the tray."

"Well! Martha, this is so sweet of you!" she said. "Billy, Buster, you're going to help me with this food. And orange juice, too. And bacon, goodness!"

There was a neatly folded blue napkin next to the plate. There was silverware. Butter, syrup. The tray did look nice. "Come on, boys!" Great-grandmother said. "Get some of my pancakes."

"Now take it easy." Thomas warned his brothers.

They took it easy. They climbed down to stand by the bed next to the tray. "Pan-*cakes*!" said Billy. "Cakes!" Buster whispered.

They stood in line. Buster was first. Great-grandmother Jeffers spread butter and syrup on the pancakes. She cut a nice piece, speared it with her fork, and held it out to Buster. He took it all in one bite. "Ummmm!" he said.

Next, Billy took his portion in two bites. "Ummmmhuuum!" he moaned happily.

"That's it, you guys," Martha said. "We have to get going. Thomas, come help me with their coats and boots."

Thomas and Pesty both helped, standing by the closet in the downstairs hall. The boys liked to grab

Pesty around the neck. With their combined weight, they could topple her to her knees.

"Goodbye! Grandmother Rhetty? We're going," Martha called up the stairs.

"Bye!" said Billy and Buster. Now in their snowsuits, they were eager to go.

"Bye, you-all, have a good time," Great-grandmother called from her room.

"Bye," Thomas said.

"Bye, y'all!" Pesty added.

Then they were gone in the car. Pesty and Thomas watched it go down the road. By the time the two of them were back upstairs, Great-grandmother Jeffers was out of bed and in her bathrobe. The breakfast tray was on the floor.

"Take the tray, please, Thomas," she said.

"But you haven't eaten hardly a thing," Thomas said.

"I know it," Great-grandmother said. "I never eat much for breakfast. You-all wait for me downstairs," she said to them. "I'll get dressed and we'll go."

"We're going to Mr. Pluto's?" Thomas asked.

"Why not? Just let me get ready!" she said.

10

"**M**aybe y'all could come over to my house, too," Pesty said shyly to Thomas.

"That would be something!" Thomas murmured. He set the tray down on the kitchen counter. He and Pesty ate the pancakes and bacon that Great-grandmother hadn't eaten. "Mama'll never know Great-grandmother Jeffers didn't have her breakfast," Thomas said. He took a pitcher of orange juice from the refrigerator and poured them tall glasses; put the pitcher back.

They sat down with the juice at the kitchen table. They drank greedily.

"Well," Thomas said when he had finished, "that's my Great-grandmother Jeffers, come to stay."

"She's a nice old lady," Pesty said.

"She always is," Thomas said.

"Bet she's a lot of fun," Pesty said.

"She gets just as excited as I do over things," Thomas said.

Sitting there, looking at the kitchen wall, he felt good about everything. Great-grandmother Jeffers brings good luck, he thought.

All at once he stiffened. He was staring at the wall that could rise. He gazed from the wall to the doorway and beyond to the front hallway and the front door at the other end. A creepy feeling light as feathers curled down his back as he remembered a weird and ghostly sighing he'd heard in the tunnel behind the kitchen wall. That was months ago, he thought.

"Mr. Thomas," Pesty said softly, "what's awrong with you, staring like that?"

He sighed. "Well, you remember the front steps and the tunnel?"

"Yeah! And you fell down in there, under the steps," she said.

"Uh-huh, and it leads to here," he said, "to the other side of this wall."

"Me and Macky just knew about it coming to an end," she said.

"That's because you can't get into here from the other side. You have to lift that wall from inside, in this kitchen," he said. "Otherwise, it looks just like the tunnel comes to an end." There's nothing behind it, he thought, looking at the wall. Slowly he got to his feet. He tiptoed over to the high cabinet opposite the tunnel wall. "I'm going to do it," he said.

"Do what?" Pesty asked.

"I'm going to raise that wall," he said.

"With your bare hands? I'd sure like to see that!" Pesty said.

Thomas laughed. "Watch the magic!" he said. He opened a cabinet drawer. The house was quiet about him, with no Billy or Buster running and banging around. It felt empty without his mama's voice rising like summer light on the air. When Thomas listened hard, he imagined he could hear the limestone earth beneath the house seeping and percolating with snow-melt.

Don't let it drip in the great cavern. Don't let it cause a cave-in.

Thomas remembered seeing his papa take a mechanism from the machinery that raised and lowered the trick wall. His papa had put the mechanism in the drawer. Thomas opened the drawer and took it out. He next looked under the base of the high cabinet above the counter. There was a hidden panel. It slid open at his touch.

Pesty was there at his side. "Wow-wee!" she whispered.

"I saw Papa do this," Thomas told her. But he had never done it himself.

Inside was the machinery for the trick wall. He placed the part in his hand in a section of the machinery where he thought it might go.

"Doesn't seem to fit," Pesty said.

"You're right. I have to look for an empty space."

"Try it here," she said, pointing.

He tried it. "No," he said, "but maybe . . . here? No. Here? Here!"

"Push the underpart in," Pesty said.

"That's where it goes. Now I'll pull the lever." Gently he pulled it.

They watched the trick wall. Pesty's eyes were huge. Her mouth gaped.

Thomas's scalp tingled as the wall rose.

"Thomaaas! Thomaaas!" A plaintive, distant voice called to him.

They were transfixed by the wall rising. The black hole of a tunnel entrance was exposed. It seemed to attack them with its damp and dark. A dank smell invaded the kitchen. But there was nothing at all that he could see beyond the tunnel opening. "Thomaaas!" came the voice again.

"Oh my goodness!" Thomas said. He flicked the lever, letting the wall slide back down.

"It's just your great mother calling from upstairs," Pesty said. But she had been frightened, too.

"I know it is," he said. Now why do you upset yourself? he thought. You were sure it was somebody calling in that tunnel. "What is it, Great-grandmother?" he hollered. "I'm coming!" He remembered to close the cabinet drawer before he rushed out of the kitchen, down the hall and up the stairs.

"Great-grandmother? I'm coming!" he called again. He bounded up the steps, taking them three at a time. Pesty was right behind him.

He rushed into Great-grandmother Jeffers's room, only to find it empty.

Where?—Thomas hurried to his room, then, the twins' room. She wasn't in either room. "Great-grandmother," he called, "where are you?"

"I'm here, Thomas," came the reply from a distance away.

"Well, man, she's in the back bedroom we never use!" Thomas said.

"In here, Thomas," he heard Great-grandmother say again.

Pesty was on her way down the hall first. "She's in this room," she said. The end of the hall was at the very rear of the upstairs.

The rear of the upstairs ended at a big window that looked out over the veranda, the rear yard, and the hill rising beyond. There was a room on either side of the hall, with windows also facing the back of the house. Thomas's folks had dusted and polished the floors and then had closed the rooms. They hadn't found any further use for them.

He opened the door, with Pesty at his elbow. At once he felt the chill air; he could smell the floor polish. There was a slight odor of stale dampness. It reminded him of the dankness that had come from the tunnel opening in the kitchen.

"What is it, Great-grandmother?" he said, coming up to her. "What are you doing in here?" She was standing facing the wall directly across from the door with her back to him. She was dressed for the day.

"Thomas," she said, reaching out across him as he came up to her, as though to shield him. "Well," she said, and sighed, "it's hard to say what it is. But it is why I am in here."

He took a step forward in order to see her face, but she pulled him back.

"You mustn't go any closer," she told him.

"Wh-why is that?" he said.

"Well. That—that . . . wall." *That floor* was what she had first thought and at once had thought better of saying it. "Er, there was someone here."

"There—there was?" Thomas managed to say, as the creeps came over him.

"Oh yes," she said. "You see, I had come out of my room into the hall. Heard you-all in the kitchen. Thought sure I felt someone behind me. I turned around, yet all I saw was an empty hall. But after talking to Martha last night, I knew how she kept the unused rooms closed because of the twins. Well, I went to close one of the doors I saw was slightly open." She sighed. "Just as I reached in to put my hand on the doorknob, someone reached out from inside that room and put a hand over mine."

Thomas sucked in his breath. "No!" he said.

Great-grandmother nodded. "Just out of nowhere, someone put a hand over mine," she repeated.

"Great-grandmother, who was it?" Thomas asked.

"Someone big, very big. That's all I know," she said. "Scared me! Almost had heart failure, too!" Great-grandmother Jeffers laughed nervously.

"Well, I came on in here. Managed to see it go— huh!" she said. "It left behind its motion, it felt like. Well. What I saw of it was the shape. A long, leggy shape, darkness. How strange! I was so taken by surprise. Who would expect something like that to happen in broad daylight?"

Silently Pesty walked around them, up to the wall.

"Pesty! Don't!" Thomas held her back, but she shook loose from his grasp.

She stood there, just where Great-grandmother had warned Thomas not to stand, and knocked on the wall, as if she were knocking at the front door downstairs.

She knocked, pong, pong, pong. It made a hollow sound. She seemed to push the wall. She knocked a second time, pong, pong, pong.

The wall began to move; the floor in front of it commenced to turn.

Thomas couldn't believe his eyes. A half circle of the floor with a section of the bedroom wall behind it was turning slowly to his right. At once Pesty stepped out of the turning part of the floor.

"You knew about this wall!" Thomas said to her.

Pesty said not a word. She stood there with her hands clasped in front of her, looking at the wall turning. The back of the wall, its other, hidden side, was coming around into view.

"It's a circle," Thomas whispered.

"And one-half of it hidden all the time," Great-grandmother said softly. "But wait . . . maybe . . . you won't believe . . ." What came around from behind was so unexpected. It was so shocking Thomas wanted to hide his face from it.

"That's it, that's what was there before," Great-grandmother said.

Pesty stood there, calmly looking up. Thomas was looking up as well. And so was Great-grandmother Jeffers. Up and up.

"Mr. Thomas," Pesty said. "Great Mother Jeffers," she said soothingly. She reached out with gentle hands for what was there, for what had come from behind the wall.

The first thing Thomas noticed was the motion Great-grandmother Jeffers spoke about. Nervous, frantic motion was what came to mind.

Pesty took a few steps to the side where there was a table and turned on the small brass lamp by a straight chair near the wall. The lamp gave off a soft glow of light.

"Mr. Thomas," Pesty said. She went back over to the turned wall. She had her hand now on the one who had come. "She didn't mean anything. Didn't mean to scare your great-grandmother."

"What?" Thomas said, barely out loud. He was staring at the one so tall.

"Y'all," Pesty said to them. "Want you to meet my mama. She wasn't following Great Mother Jeffers down the hall. It's just that this house was hers to wander before y'all ever came to live here.

"But don't move too sudden," Pesty continued. "Mama not too well, though she up and around again."

Thomas and Great-grandmother Jeffers simply stared. The place that had turned had a handsome stone fireplace with a marble mantel. The woman stood on the wide hearth, crouched a bit, leaning her back against the mantel.

"Oh!" Thomas said. He realized then that she wasn't a giant, as he had thought. She was about six inches off the floor up on the raised stone hearth. But she was still big and tall, probably the tallest, the biggest, and the most different woman Thomas had ever seen. She sent out a powerful magnetism. It was as if electricity surrounded her. He could almost feel its prickly current. It wasn't possible. But there it was.

11

Mrs. Darrow had thick black hair that fanned out over her shoulders to cascade down her back, below her waist. The long dress she wore was a worn and shabby tent cinched at the waist. It had a neck hole and holes for her hands out of the long sleeves gathered at her wrists. It had heavily padded shoulders as stiff and flat as boards. It looked like a shelter of cloth stretched over her huge figure from neck to ankles. She wore it like a protective armor. She might have been five feet eleven inches or even over six feet tall, Thomas supposed. And she might have weighed two hundred, three hundred pounds, he couldn't be sure. But she didn't look fat. Just big.

Thomas couldn't take his eyes off her. He knew that only seconds had passed, that Pesty had spoken, introducing her mama. But he couldn't find any words in his head. He was just so struck by her. Enormous Mrs. Darrow, standing over him.

She had her arms crossed over her chest so that they made a wide X, with her hands touching her shoulders. Her eyes were like two black, burning lights stuck to her face. Her mouth was a thin line with great creases at either side. She might have been smiling. But she was not. She was staring. Her black eyes fastened on Thomas.

Something else, Thomas thought. I hear . . . humming!

She was humming and had been humming, like a soft buzzing from the time she had come around from behind the wall. The humming had buzzed inside his head, as if it had belonged there. He hadn't noticed it until now.

"Can't you say hello to my mama?" Pesty was asking him.

"Oh, oh, hello! I'm sorry, Mrs. Darrow, I was . . . shoot. Hello!" Thomas said.

"Thomas and I are glad to meet you, Mrs. Darrow."

Great-grandmother Jeffers finally spoke, in a natural, soothing voice, not too loud.

The humming did not cease. Great-grandmother took a step forward and extended her palm in greeting. Mrs. Darrow swung her head around toward Great-grandmother. Eyes, burning black fire, glinting so, that Great-grandmother drew back; she could not help herself. It was clear the woman was awfully, terribly different.

At once Pesty stepped between her mother and Great-grandmother. Mrs. Darrow had dropped her arms. Her hands clenched into fists.

"Great Mother Jeffers, you got to move slow, please," Pesty said. "See, my mama is all right, once you know what to do and what not to do."

Pesty had hold of her mother's hands, fists. She rubbed and rubbed at them until Mrs. Darrow relaxed them a bit, opening them partway.

"She can't help herself," Pesty said simply. "Doctor calls it something." She started again, carefully. "Doctor says she is ill, mental. She is chronic. See, that means it comes and goes."

"Chronic," Great-grandmother said softly. "Did she take her medicine today?" she added, gazing back at the black eyes that froze on her now.

"She might not've," Pesty said. "Well, how did you know she might've forgot?" She was surprised that Great-grandmother Jeffers would think of that.

"Mama might not've, with me run off to go around with Mr. Thomas."

"Well, then we'll take her back and see that she gets her medicine and gets warmed up," Great-grandmother said. "I suspect that the way she came was chilly."

Thomas couldn't believe he'd heard right.

"Thomas," she continued, "go get my shawl for Mrs. Darrow to put on, please—move slowly now, we don't want to upset her—and get my coat and hat for me. My scarf. Don't want to catch my death. You might do well to bring a flashlight, too."

The humming ceased suddenly. "Sooky," Mrs. Darrow murmured. Her voice was strangely clear and childlike, not at all like the sound of her humming.

"What did she say?" Thomas asked, trying not to move even his lips.

"She always says that for a few days," Pesty said. "Sooky. That's what she calls me when she starts in talking again. See, when she is sick, she won't call me at all. She will sit in one place forever unless somebody move her. She don't want to eat until she comes out of it. And then she eat everything in sight."

"Great-grandmother . . ."

"Thomas," Great-grandmother said, "we'll go back there with her, see that she's fine. Oh, and how about one of the pies in the refrigerator? Yes! Just bring it on up here."

"But you don't know what went on," Thomas said quickly. "Her sons . . . what they did to the kitchen." He glanced up at Mrs. Darrow and away before she could swing her eyes at him. "I don't think Papa—"

"Thomas," Great-grandmother interrupted, "I heard about some of what went on here when you-all first come months ago. Well, your papa is my grandson, so don't you worry. Hurry now, Thomas," she said. "We don't want to keep Mrs. Darrow waiting!"

She smiled bravely at him and all around. Great-grandmother was going to help Mrs. Darrow even though she was a little afraid of her. Thomas could tell.

He hurried downstairs to the closet. First, he grabbed his and Pesty's coats from the backs of chairs in the kitchen. He stuffed a flashlight in his jacket pocket. Then he got the pie. He didn't know what kind it was; it was wrapped in foil in the refrigerator. It was probably apple. He hurried to the hall, placed the pie carefully on the floor, and laid their coats next to it. Then he got Great-grandmother's things from the closet. The shawl, too. Oh man! It's taking me too long!

But he hurried. Careful to hold the pie with both hands. He had his own coat and hat on now. He had Pesty's coat draped over his head and down his back. He had Great-grandmother's things and her shawl over one arm. He did not know whether what they were about to do was safe or sane. Another secret opening into the house right upstairs! he was thinking.

A crazy woman? She is Pesty's mama. Mrs. Darrow. Wonder what is her first name? You could ask.

When he returned, he stopped still just in the door-way to the bedroom. He pulled the pie rim in tightly against him. The flashlight weighted him down on one side. Mrs. Darrow had stepped down from the fire-place hearth. She stood over Great-grandmother Jeffers. She had hold of her own long hair in one hand and Great-grandmother's in the other. She was pulling Great-grandmother's hair as she pulled her own. She looked like a giant bully bothering tiny Great-grand-mother Jeffers.

"Mr. Thomas, don't say nothing," Pesty said, before he could think to say anything. "Don't make to inter-fere."

"But look!" Thomas said, coming in very slowly. He spoke as calmly as he could. "She is hurting my great-grandmother." He calculated how fast he could get to Great-grandmother's side and how much he could do for her once he was there.

"She's not hurting me, Thomas," Great-grand-mother said, "not really." She reached up, hoping to loosen Mrs. Darrow's grip on her hair. But she couldn't.

"Mama don't realize how strong she is," Pesty said. "I think she means to shake your hand, Mother Jeffers, but she got it wrong—see? She shaking your hair."

Pesty pried her mother's hands loose. "She's my

mama when she goes off her mind," she said, "but she comes back like a child. Sorry, Great Mother."

"It's all right," Great-grandmother said, "I'm not hurt."

"Once Mama is up out of bed, she has to learn most things all over again," Pesty explained.

"Think of that!" Great-grandmother whispered.

"Why is that?" Thomas asked. Slowly he moved up to them. He put the pie down on the lamp table and reached over to give Pesty Great-grandmother's shawl. Pesty took it and flung it up around her mama's shoulders.

"She says she don't remember much after," Pesty said. "Then we give her her pills. They help her get better, but they make it hard for her to remember, too."

"But does this . . ." Thomas began. He was going to ask, Does it go on forever? Didn't her mama ever get better? But he never got the chance.

With no warning Mrs. Darrow swung around toward him. That unheard-of nervous motion seemed to hit him between the eyes. She lunged for the pie, knocking Thomas aside. He fell on the floor hard.

Thomas sat there, stunned, watching Mrs. Darrow. A dull ache began along his hip, where he'd hit.

Mrs. Darrow lifted the pie up to her nose. She tore at the foil covering and threw it aside. There was the pie; it was apple. He wouldn't have dreamed the pie would get eaten the way he saw her eating it. With one hand Mrs. Darrow commenced to scoop the pie.

Thomas suddenly was angry. "She pushed me down!" he said. Fury mixed with the bruising fall.

"Mama didn't mean to, Mr. Thomas. You just got in the way," Pesty said back.

"She hit into me; she shoved me and knocked me *down*," he said.

"No, *you* got in *her* way! You did, you got in her *way!*" Pesty's voice shook. Trembling, she covered her face with her hands.

Mrs. Darrow finished about half the pie. Her mouth and cheeks were a sticky mess with it.

Pesty commenced sobbing.

"Pesty, I'm—I'm sorry," Thomas said, getting up. "But she did push me down."

"Now, don't you cry, sweetheart," Great-grandmother said. She folded Pesty in her arms.

Pesty's crying lasted only a few seconds. She had little time for tears. "Mama, come on," she said. Sighing, she went to her mother and calmly took the pie out of her hands. It was almost all gone. "Take you on back home now. You played enough for today."

"Don't cry, Sooky!" Mrs. Darrow said. Her calm, reasonable voice surprised them.

Thomas wouldn't say that the expression under the sticky mess on her face was a smile. But her mouth was

open, and her teeth were showing. He supposed it was
a smile to soothe Pesty.

"Ha-ha," Mrs. Darrow said. "Hey? Sooky!"

"It's okay, Mama. We'll be back home in a minute,"
Pesty told her.

"How do we make that wall swing around?" asked
Great-grandmother Jeffers.

"You have to follow us," Pesty said. She was leading
her mother, wrapped in Great-grandmother's shawl,
back to the wall. "You climb on up and stand on the
side of the fireplace. Then you push on a place
here. . . ." Thomas watched her push at a section of
the mantel. A square of stone seemed to move inward
about a quarter of an inch. "Then you just stand still,"
Pesty continued. "The wall seem to tilt back some. . . ."
She and her mother stood on the hearth. Slowly the
wall swung around, scraping a little as it went. "Mr.
Thomas, y'all come on." They were gone around to the
other side.

"Come on, Thomas," Great-grandmother Jeffers
said, hurrying into her coat. "Now I'm a little old and a
bit unsteady, so you must help me up on that hearth."

Thomas sighed. "Are you sure you want to do this,
Great-grandmother?"

"It will be all right," she said firmly.

Thomas helped her up onto the hearth. She held on
to his arm as he reached behind him to press the mantel. It took him a moment to find the right place.

"Little farther over, I think, Thomas," Great-grand-mother said.

"Right," he said. This time he pushed and a mantel stone gave way. The wall, the fireplace, and the hearth where they stood began to move. He hardly dared breathe. What will there be on the other side? he wondered as the two of them went slowly around.

12

I t's tricky, he thought. Step off the wall around back there, and you don't know where you are. Shine the flashlight, and there's the steepest staircase right inside the bedroom wall. Think of it! You go down the stairs below the foundation of the house. It's so dark, and you guess you're in a tunnel. It smells earth-musty like a tunnel. Shine the light around. Yes, it's a tunnel, leading away from the house. And you walk a ways. Hold on to Great-grandmother.

Don't lose her in the dark! It feels like you turn a corner, and then—

He and Great-grandmother Jeffers had completed all the steps that he'd just gone over in his mind. Putting them in order helped him make sense out of what had come next. Now they followed Pesty and her mother to an unbelievable place. "It's—it's a—a—whole decorated room!" Thomas exclaimed, shining his light around. The tunnel had seemed to widen, and in the open space was indeed a room.

"But it's different; it's made to be another time," Great-grandmother said. "Oh, it's so pretty!"

And so it was. The room seemed all dark, carved wood of the bedstead, chiffonier, and side chair. Thomas flicked his light. There was a silken coverlet on the bed. There were end tables with taffeta skirts. On one end table there were bottles, one blue, one green, glowing richly in his light. Seeing them so suddenly, he felt as if they had stumbled upon familiar ground.

Then Pesty lit a brass oil lantern on one of the tables. Thomas and Great-grandmother Jeffers could well see that the items in the room were of great value. Why would anyone want to put a fine room like this in the middle of a tunnel? Thomas wondered.

"We're going on now," Pesty said. "You can see it all when you come back."

"Pesty, you knew about this secret room, too, and you never told me?" Thomas asked.

"It's just where my mama will come to sit. Wasn't nothing to tell. Come on, I got to get her on home before the mens come back from working."

The men. Darrow men. "Great-grandmother, I think we should go on back," Thomas began. "No telling what we . . ." He didn't finish.

Great-grandmother Jeffers had taken him by the hand and led him along as if he were a little child, following Pesty. Pesty opened a door at the other end of the room, just as though she were opening the door leading into the front hallway of the Drear house. Only, with this door, she simply pulled on it. It lurched toward her. Then she took hold of it and pushed it to the side. There were no hinges on it, Thomas realized. He saw a gaping black space where the door had been.

"Mr. Thomas, when you come back, put the door in place from the inside," she told him.

"Don't you worry, Pesty," Great-grandmother said. "We'll take care of it."

Now there began more of the tunnel. The room had been just like a wide place in a road, Thomas thought. "Do you feel funny, Great-grandmother?" he asked as softly as he could.

"Funny about what?" she said.

"About . . . being here. Finding the room. Don't you feel it should be left the way it is, without us getting into it?"

"Well, Thomas, everywhere you walk, you are walking into *it*, into history, so to speak," she said. "Always somebody's walked before you. Something's gone on with people before we were thought of. We can't help that. And here Mrs. Darrow has found comfort in the history of that room, I suspect. It fits her mind, like the twists of the tunnels do.

"But I understand what you mean, Thomas," Great-grandmother added. "It makes you feel foolish, walking around underground." She chuckled. "It makes you want to bust out laughing. Who'd ever think of such a thing? But it makes you feel good, too, down here. Because you feel close to those who ran long ago, like you are tracing the footsteps of fugitives with your own feet."

"Maybe so," Thomas murmured. When we come back, I'll take a good look, he thought. Funny, to put a door there. But I guess someone did want it to look like a room. Who do you suppose? Do I tell Papa about this?

The tunnel was deeply dark. Thomas's flashlight was dim in the blackness. He could see Pesty's back, but he couldn't see Mrs. Darrow. The tunnel turned and snaked. They had to walk single file. Great-grandmother Jeffers was behind Thomas. He held on to her hand now, leading her. The ceiling was perhaps six feet from the floor, barely high enough for Pesty's mother.

"You forgot and left that lantern burning back there, Pesty," Thomas called.

"Didn't forget," she said. Her voice seemed to be

right next to his ear. Tunnels could do that, could throw back and echo sound. "Turn it off when you go back," she said. "It has a knob that you just turn and the flame goes out. I'll let you do that," she said.

He thought her tone of voice sounded different somehow. "You could burn up that room, leaving the light on," he told her. "Look, where are we going? Where does this tunnel lead?"

Pesty's giggle was all tinkly in his ear. "Mr. Thomas, you are so funny! I told you, I got to take my mama home."

"Oh," he said. Well, she had told him. Of course, they were going over to the Darrows. He just didn't want to think about it.

"It's going to be too far for you, Great-grandmother," he said.

"Thomas, I'm doing all right," she said. "I've got my coat and hat on, too. It's not snowing on me in here; it's not icy either. Long as I have hold of you, I can't fall. Just keep on. I'll be fine."

"Pesty, how much farther?" he said as casually as he could. He didn't want to disturb Mrs. Darrow there in the darkness.

"You sure are in a hurry." There came Pesty's delicate laughter again. "We'll be there in a little while."

They walked on. He thought of Mr. Pluto and how it happened he couldn't take Great-grandmother to see him today.

Then they walked through standing water. "Did you get your feet too wet?" He asked Great-grandmother.

"No, no," she said. "My feet are just fine."

In a short time Thomas and Great-grandmother came up behind Pesty and Mrs. Darrow. The tunnel dead-ended. Set in the cave end was a makeshift door made from pieces of wood. Pesty placed the side of her head up against the door. Mrs. Darrow did the same, murmuring a meaningless sound of words.

"Pesty!"

"Shhhh, Mr. Thomas!" Pesty whispered. "We got to listen."

They listened. And Thomas and Great-grandmother Jeffers stood still in the dark, about to jump out of their skins. Thomas had flicked out the light, for whoever could be on the other side of the door might see it. No telling what surrounded them in the blackness either. Spirits of the dead. The living, maybe, about to drag them off somewhere in the maze of tunnels.

"It's okay," finally Pesty said. Her voice remained low. "Come on, Mama." Mrs. Darrow was humming now to herself. The sound was not unpleasant.

Guess she is happy, Thomas thought. I sure hope she is.

Pesty pushed on the door, and it slid to the right. There was enough light to see that there were clothes hanging.

"The back of a closet," whispered Great-grand-mother Jeffers.

"What?" said Thomas.

"You walk in the closet, and you walk out the closet. That's it," Pesty told him. She led her mother inside, pushing the clothing over to make way. Great-grand-mother and Thomas followed.

Thomas paused, let Great-grandmother by. His heart thumped in his chest. "Do I close this—this opening?" he asked.

"Yes," Pesty said.

He closed the back of the closet, sliding it into place with his hands. And he walked through the hanging clothes; then he pushed them into place again. No one would ever know there was a hidden door to a tunnel behind them.

This is the queerest day I've ever lived through, and it's not even over yet. Can you believe what we're doing? he thought. And that Mrs. Darrow? What would Papa say about her? Ohhhh don't think.

Pesty led her mother to a brass bed across the room from the closet.

"My mama's bedroom," Pesty said, seeing Thomas and Great-grandmother looking wide-eyed all around. The brass bed shone with a pink glow. "Mama stays here most of the time." She took her mother's shoes off and helped her under the covers. She arranged the shawl around her. "Me and Macky will walk her some," Pesty explained, "but not in the wintertime. In the snow time Macky don't know she walks. She will walk in the tunnels, then, and nobody know about that but me."

Pesty poured water from a pitcher on the end table into a glass. She gave Mrs. Darrow the pills she'd forgotten. Mrs. Darrow took her pills, drank the water, and at last sank down against her pillows. Pesty washed the stickiness from her mother's face.

"Where *is* Macky?" Thomas asked. He was happy to be back in a house, even if it was the Darrow house, and out of the forbidding tunnel.

"Couldn't say," Pesty said. "Maybe he's home. Keep your voice down. Don't want them to know somebody's here."

"Who don't you want to know?" Thomas asked.

"Anybody. Wouldn't do, if someone's in the house. How'm I going to explain something like that?" Pesty said. "If you speak low, they think she is just talking with me or to herself."

"You mean . . ." Thomas began.

"She means, nobody knows about that tunnel but her and Mrs. Darrow," Great-grandmother Jeffers said. "How would she explain our being here when no one saw us come in from the outside? Isn't that right, Pesty?"

Pesty nodded. She wet a towel in the washbasin. She wiped her own shoes off from the tunnel wet and dirt, then Mrs. Darrow's. She handed the towel to Thomas. He cleaned off his and Great-grandmother's shoes.

"Thank you, Thomas," Great-grandmother Jeffers said. He handed Pesty back the towel; she put it in a hamper next to the stand.

Pesty patted Mrs. Darrow's pillows. Her mother lay on her back, straight as an arrow, staring at Thomas. Now and then she would nod for no reason that Thomas could see.

"Once upon a time," Mrs. Darrow said, grinning at him.

"She's going to tell a story," he whispered to Pesty.

"She might and she might not," Pesty said. "Sometimes she will."

Great-grandmother Jeffers sat in an old easy chair by the head of the bed.

They spoke in quiet voices so that Mrs. Darrow would stay calm and so they would not be overheard. Thomas settled in a straight chair on the other side, toward the foot of the bed. "Macky told me she likes to tell old kinds of stories," he said.

"Is that so?" said Great-grandmother Jeffers.

"Uh-huh," he said. "There's one about an Indian maiden he told."

Mrs. Darrow sat bolt upright in bed. Her black eyes glared at Thomas.

"Shhh! Mr. Thomas, don't you say nothing about *that*!" Pesty said.

"What, the Indian maiden?" Thomas asked before he thought.

Mrs. Darrow commenced climbing out of the bed.

"What a pretty shawl! You like that pretty shawl, Mama!" Pesty said in a loud whisper. "Great-grand-mother Jeffers, you want it back today?"

"Why, no, dear, you let your mama wear it as long as she wants to. She seems to like it."

Distracted by talk of the shawl, Mrs. Darrow grabbed hold of it to wrap it more tightly around her. She climbed back into bed.

Thomas was amazed at how fast she could move. What would she have done to him? he wondered. He gazed at her long, thick hair and then, around the room, just so she wouldn't think he was staring. There was a picture on the wall opposite him. He couldn't quite make it out.

They say Indian hair is like hers. So there is native ancestry on the mother's side? he thought. He re-minded himself that Darrow men were descended partly from Indians, too. River Ross, River Lewis . . . He recalled that it was River Thames said to have come here with Dies Drear. Do you suppose—

"What is your mama's name?" he asked Pesty, barely moving his lips. Pesty was there in front of him, sitting on the bed, holding her mama's hand.

Before she could speak, Mrs. Darrow spoke. "I sit with my feet on the right," she said.

"Mama, come on now," Pesty said, patting her hand. She glanced around apologetically. "When she's feeling better, she likes to talk," she said.

"Call me Eater," Mrs. Darrow said in a disjointed,

detached voice. "Hunters brought back plenty food. I will eat anythin'." She laughed hugely.

Thomas and Great-grandmother Jeffers were bewildered.

"Mr. Thomas, don't say nothing," Pesty said, casually. "She's telling something, maybe talking about the—" Pesty mouthed the words "Indian maiden."

"When they were together one time," Mrs. Darrow murmured, "she told Brave Wolf, 'If you dare to beat me again, I will fight you. I don't care if you kill me.' After that moment he was ever her slave."

"She's just talking," Pesty said happily. "Guess just snatches of stories."

"From October until June," Mrs. Darrow murmured, "October till June." She closed her eyes and appeared to go to sleep.

"She's in the October-June phase now," said a voice. "She's not just talking."

Thomas jumped up and spun around, almost toppling the chair he had been sitting on. There stood Mac Darrow. How long he had been there Thomas couldn't say. Macky was like a tall, dark shadow, holding the door open with his shoulder. Now he came up to stand at Thomas's side. He still had the outdoors about him, and a musty scent, too. He looked dusty. He put a dirt-smeared hand on the back of the chair. "You—you want to sit down?" Thomas asked, and moved out of his way.

Macky sat down. Nodded at his sleeping mama and

Pesty. He stood up again, absently, to greet Great-grandmother Jeffers. Pesty told him who Great-grandmother was, that she and Thomas had walked over to visit. Then, looking exhausted, Macky sat down again.

Great-grandmother Jeffers smiled. She regarded Mac Darrow, but she didn't say anything to him. His hair was gray with dirt and dust. His face, his clothes were damp and soiled. He's been hunting underground, she realized. What a peculiar family, all the time scurrying in the dark.

They were silent, watching Macky. Thomas felt a keen sympathy for him. Macky looked beaten. Sort of like he's sick of . . . himself, Thomas thought.

Pesty frowned at Thomas and Great-grandmother. Slowly it dawned on him that the frown was a warning: Keep still. Don't give anything away to Macky. Why? Thomas wondered. He's on our side, isn't he? Well, you wouldn't know it by the way he tricked me in the woods. He's still a Darrow, and don't forget it.

There was a long silence. Macky studied his mother's sleeping face. In sleep she didn't look at all odd or crazy, Thomas noted. "I got lost," Macky said abruptly. "Fell into a hole by accident." Smirking. "Been lost for three hours. Never thought I'd see the light of day."

13

"Lost? What hole? " Pesty said. "You know Daddy says not to go wandering around. That's how you get lost. Not minding. You not mind, a tunnel will fall in on you one time."

Pesty surprised Thomas. She seemed to him even more upset than what she said to Macky showed. She walked the tunnels. But then she did know where she was going.

"Are there many tunnels?" asked Great-grand-mother.

"*I* don't know," Pesty said. "*I'm* not allowed to play around in them." She gazed hard, warning, at Thomas and Great-grandmother.

She's hiding everything from Macky. I don't like it, Thomas thought. What if he found out? Maybe that's why he's been exploring underground. He didn't fall into a hole. He could've gone in the same way Pesty and I did into Pluto's cave. Maybe he's the someone got in there, trying to find out something.

Macky ignored Pesty. He was staring at his mama. "If you forget what you're doing for a minute, you can get lost," he said with sadness. "If you get scared and panic, you'll never find your way back."

Is he talking about himself or his mama? Thomas wondered.

"You want to sit down?" Macky asked Thomas po-litely.

"No, thank you," Thomas said, pleased that Macky remembered he was there.

"You must not have panicked down there then, young man," said Great-grandmother Jeffers, "else you wouldn't be among us."

"No, ma'am, I didn't," Mac Darrow said. "But when I couldn't find my way, I thought I'd never get out." He studied space at the foot of the bed.

"You were lucky," said Great-grandmother.

Silence, like a storm gathering, surrounded them. Pesty looked doubtfully at Macky; he stared defiantly at the floor.

Mrs. Darrow opened her eyes. Grinning, she greeted her son. "Mac, Macs, Ha-ha. Make tracks. Let's go hunting. Ha-ha."

Forlornly Macky smiled. He leaned over, kissed his mama's cheek. Thomas never would've believed big Mac Darrow could do something so tender.

He turned to them and explained. "Mama, talking about travelin' in the October-June time, like the season is now. Talking about a hundred, hundred fifty years ago. She must've heard tales. Just bits and pieces, I guess. If you listen good, you might can figure it. Sometimes I think I know, but then I don't know."

"Figure what?" Pesty said suspiciously.

"Figure out the time when the people had to separate each fall, and in winter and spring, too," Macky said. "They couldn't all stay in one place and feed everybody and all the horses. So they had to part company. But in the summer the bands got back together for the hunt or maybe to fight an enemy."

"Your mama is—are you talking about—about Indians?" Thomas said.

"She'll talk about sitting on the right. That's the way most of the tribewomen sat, although I don't know which tribe," Macky said. "And which must mean some other women sat with their feet on the left, I guess."

"Oh, shoot. Mama don't mean nothing by that stuff!" Pesty said.

Said too quickly, it seemed to Great-grandmother Jeffers. She watched Pesty and then Macky and listened intently. It's all mixed up, but it makes sense, too, she was thinking. Here we have a brother and sister at odds. Each has a piece of some lost puzzle. Pesty knows much. Macky is trying to discover.

"The Indian . . ." Thomas started to say "maiden" but remembered not to. At the same moment the picture on the wall across from him caught his attention.

Macky nodded with regard to the Indian maiden. "She's hightailing it in all the stories. She's running away, either from someone trying to run faster," he said, "or from somethin' else."

Thomas listened while looking at the picture on the wall over there. There was something about it.

"And what Mama said about being an Eater. Well," Macky said, "my Daddy says the Eaters was a band of Indians, and a band has related kin."

The picture! Thomas was thinking. Look at it!

"But what does she care about that? She ain't a Indian!" Pesty said.

"Well, who knows why?" Macky replied. "She sometimes tells about her people here, don't you, Mama?"

spoken gently to his mother. "Been here for ages. Wasn't just Daddy's people was part natives."

"Who cares?" Pesty said, like a smart aleck.

I can't just go over and look at the picture, can I? Thomas thought. "That's a nice picture over there. Can I see it?" he said. He went slowly around the bed, so as not to disturb Mrs. Darrow. He acted only casually interested in the picture. It didn't look like anything much up close. He didn't know too much about painting. But he knew this was the kind you could buy ready-made in the dime store. It had a beige sky and a deeper brown earth. It looked somber.

I bet I could do that good, he thought. A horseman out in a track of land was what it was. There was a mean homestead to the horseman's back and a rocky trail in the foreground. Then he felt Mac Darrow right behind him.

"What do you think you're doing?" Macky spoke low, whispering in his ear.

"Looking at the picture," Thomas said evenly. "I bet I could almost copy it, too."

"Didn't know you were some painter," Macky said, his voice a menace.

"I'm not," Thomas said. "But this looks like a piece of sculpture. I mean, look at the thick paint of the figure. Shouldn't be that hard to carve the figure in one piece." He didn't care whether Macky believed him or not.

Maybe he thinks I'm on to something, Thomas thought. Else why did he come up behind me so fast? He's *afraid* I'm on to something, if he knows what's here.

Because it wasn't the painting that had caught Thomas's eye, to pull him up so fast out of his seat. It was two corners of the picture frame. Two triangles opposite each other, made up two of the four frame corners. Two right triangles with legs of wood, forming two right angles. The solid mass areas between the angles and their hypotenuses were almost entirely hidden under the painting. But the thin edges of the hypotenuses gave off a slight glint when he moved his head back and forth.

The picture frame triangles were probably the same as the ones the Darrows had made themselves and had placed in doorframes of the Drear house months ago. By that trick the Smalls suspected Darrows meant to show them that they could secretly enter the Drear house whenever they chose. They meant to frighten Thomas's family into fleeing the house, and they had almost succeeded.

Mr. Pluto first told Thomas and his father that during slavery, triangles had been a cross reading for escaping slaves. Where a triangle fit in one of the four positions on the Greek cross would give the direction a running slave was to travel. If a triangle fit on the cross in the top left quadrant above the plane, or northwest, then the direction would be north. If it fit in the southeast quadrant, or lower right below the plane, then the direction would be south, and so on.

These two triangles are to be hidden forever in that picture frame, Thomas thought. But why? His heart quickened. I saw them fast because I know about triangles. Macky looked surprised out in the woods when I mentioned the triangles in the house. He didn't know about them! Or maybe he knew about just these two in the picture. He wouldn't know his mama wandered the house. But where would Mrs. Darrow get these triangles? And why do they glint yellow? . . . Does Macky think they are gold? Could they be? That's it! *That's* what Macky's hunting! He knows about these two in the picture frame. He figures they might be gold. There might be more somewhere, and if he finds them, he'll have treasure for his daddy and his brothers! That's why he's trying to find out something from Mr. Pluto. I bet that's it.

Have to get out of here, wait for Papa to come home.

Thomas had been thinking quickly. Macky was still breathing down his neck, leaning around him to watch his expression. Thomas kept himself calm.

"Mr. Thomas, you like that picture?" Pesty came up to stand at his side. Macky eased off a little. "My mama made it," she said, proudly.

"You mean, she painted it?" Thomas said.

"Uh-huh," Pesty said. "She used to paint. Same picture all the time. But this the only one she ever put a frame to. Made the frame herself, too."

Macky stumbled away.

"Mac, Macs, ha-ha," Mrs. Darrow murmured.

He slipped out of the room without saying goodbye to anyone.

Must be real sad to have a mama who is crazy, Thomas thought, and regretted the thought. Macky loves his mama, and she cares for him. You can tell.

Pesty was looking at him. Does she know about these triangles hidden in the picture? he wondered. Does she know why they're hidden; can she see the glinting? He wanted to say, "Pesty, what are they doing there?" But something held him back. Instead, he said, "Triangles, right triangles." Testing her.

"What, Mr. Thomas? Try what?" she said.

"Never mind," he said, not quite believing she didn't know. He was beginning to believe she knew a lot more than she was telling.

Thomas's mouth was dry. He sighed and swallowed. "Where'd Macky go?"

"Heard him go outside," Pesty said.

"Then now's the time to skedaddle," he said. "Hey! Where'd Great-grandmother go?" Just that moment she came back in through the door. "Where'd you go?" he asked. "Where've you been?"

"I went out to see who's coming, just after Macky

left. Thomas, I believe the misters are coming. We'd better get on back the way we came."

Mrs. Darrow was up on one elbow, leaning forward toward Thomas and Pesty.

"Get gone!" she said. "My horse, get away!"

"She don't want anyone close up to her picture too much, Mr. Thomas," Pesty said. "She must've woke up and seen you."

"I'm going, I'm getting away, Mrs. Darrow," he said softly. "Great-grandmother, let's go."

"Yes," Great-grandmother said. "Mrs. Darrow, we'll come to see you again sometime. We'll be real neighbors one day." She smiled kindly on the sick woman.

Mrs. Darrow stared at them with her black, burning eyes. "I'm an old-time gardener," she said. "I sit on the right side. Forever."

"Yes, indeed," said Great-grandmother. "Goodbye now, dear. We'll see you soon. Maybe take a walk with you."

"Take a walk!" said Mrs. Darrow, and she laughed uproariously.

Thomas led Great-grandmother Jeffers through the closet and into the tunnel.

"I'm going with you," said Pesty. They heard a door slam in the house just as Pesty slid the closet door closed.

"You don't have to come," Thomas whispered. "Maybe you should stay with your mother, see that she doesn't make a slip."

"They don't pay attention to her," said Pesty. "She's probably already asleep again. Here, I'll lead." She squeezed by Thomas and Great-grandmother.

"Let's go!" Thomas said.

"Give her the flashlight," Great-grandmother said.

"No, ma'am, let Mr. Thomas hold the light," Pesty said. "So's you-all can see the way. I don't need no light."

Be glad to get back to the house, Thomas thought, relieved that Pesty was leading them. So much to tell Papa! Hope he and Mama won't be mad at me. Lucky! I've got Great-grandmother on my side.

14

Who would have thought the little fellows could be so rambunctious? That Mrs. Small, her arms full of groceries in the kitchen, would have a moment's distraction. Often now the boys got away from her, running off like two wild pups. They were only going upstairs to see Great-grandmother and Thomas. And probably Pesty was with Thomas still as well.

Shortly before, Mrs. Small had stepped up onto the

front veranda and instructed Billy to take her key from her purse.

"Want to see Gray-grahma!" Billy had said, finding the key for his mama.

"Well, you'll see her in a moment," Mrs. Small had answered. She took the key, braced the groceries in her arms, and turned the key in the lock. "Now push, Buster," she had told her stoutest little son. They had entered the hall, and she'd called, "Grandmother Rhetty, we're home!" She thought she heard faint talking upstairs as she went on to the kitchen to set the bags down and put the groceries away.

She was thinking about how the boys seemed to like the nursery school. They could attend six half days or three full days a week. She thought she'd let them try it. I'll talk it over with Walter. She thought of Thomas and Mac Darrow then and smiled to herself. With the twins in school, Thomas would have more time to make new friends.

Walter came home before she could gather the boys and go pick him up. He'd gotten a ride from someone at the college. Had his papers and books, his briefcase. "We stopped at the store," he said in greeting.

Martha smiled. "Walter, I shopped, too," she said. "I bought hamburger and chicken and cookies."

"Chicken and lamb chops and cookies," he said. "Well, hello!"

"Well, we can use everything," she said.

Just then Thomas bounded down the stairs. "Papa,

Mama, you will never guess in the world what happened!" he exclaimed.

"Thomas, is Great-grandmother coming?" his mama said, thinking her little boys must have Grandmother Rhetty in tow.

"I'm right here!" Great-grandmother Jeffers called. "I'm just not so fast." Martha Small imagined that Billy and Buster were on either side of her, helping her carefully down.

But who would have thought the two little fellows would be in the exact spot to see something of what Thomas said their folks would never guess? Billy and Buster had got away from their mama when she came in with her arms full of groceries. They climbed upstairs in search of Great-grandmother, only to find her bedroom empty. They'd stood there for a moment, peeking in at the clutter.

"Gray-grahma," Billy said, "not here."

It was Buster who ran over to Thomas's room, to find that she was not there either. Together the boys went to their own room. Finding it empty, they closed the door behind them. Billy banged on the door. "Come in?" he said, imitating the way his mother answered whenever they knocked on her door.

"Come in?" Buster mimicked. They giggled.

Billy ran down the hall, knocking on closed doors. "Come in? Come in? How you do? Yes. Tank you. Please." Peals of laughter from the boys. Inspired,

Buster banged on the very last door, and it swung slowly open.

"Oooh," Billy whispered. Buster put his arm around him. Billy wrapped his arm around Buster. They stood there, looking in at the darkened bedroom. They couldn't remember ever being in this room before. Just a bedroom. They strutted in like marchers they'd seen at Street Fair Day. They didn't remember what the day was called. But they remembered the band playing, the smell of popcorn. How remarkable it was that their nearly identical minds would sort out the same experiences for both to remember! They grinned twin grins and jumped up on the bed. They stepped high across and up and down the striped bedspread.

Until the moment they heard muffled sounds there, coming from the bedroom wall where there was a fireplace. Talking, getting closer, louder, from behind the wall. Without hesitation they hid themselves. They slid off the bed to the floor behind. In the shadows of the corner there, they hid and watched, peeking under the bed. Buster crawled under, and Billy followed, scooting on his stomach up beside his brother. They held each other's hand. And looked out from beneath the bedspread that hung a couple of inches above the floor.

They saw the fireplace move around. And there were Thomas and Gray-grahma being carried slowly from the other side. Well, this must be some game.

Hiding behind a wall. Hide-and-seek! They knew not to laugh. They knew how to play.

Billy covered his mouth to keep in the giggle that was bubbling up inside him. So did Buster, as Thomas helped Great-grandmother Jeffers down from the fireplace hearth.

"Whew!" they heard Gray-grahma say. "Nice to be back inside, Thomas, isn't it?"

"It sure is," Thomas said. He turned back to the wall with the fireplace that had brought them into the room. As he pushed the place there above the mantel, the fireplace moved, went slowly around, and disappeared. And the one that had been there when the boys came in swung around again.

A slow grin spread over Billy's face.

"I hear Mama downstairs!" Thomas said. "She's home!" And he could also hear his papa's low rumble of a voice.

Thomas ran out of the room, yelling for his papa and his mama all the way. His brothers, wide-eyed under the bed, listened and waited.

Great-grandmother Jeffers went out, breathing somewhat hard now. It had been quite a walk she'd taken. She closed the door behind her.

The boys still could hear Thomas. Heard him holler, ". . . you will never guess in the world . . ." They were all alone. Peeking from under the bed, Billy watched the bottom of the closed door. But nobody came back to find him and Buster. This was hide-and-seek, so they waited for a moment longer.

Finally Buster scooted out from under the bed. Billy followed. "Shoot," Buster said. "Find us? Come in?" he added, grinning.

Billy didn't want to play knock, knock, come in. He knew where there was another game. He looked at the fireplace for a long time. Buster came up next to him. He looked over at the fireplace and back to Billy.

There was a long, silent moment. Billy grinned from ear to ear again. He put his arm around his brother. "Merry-go-*round*!" he said.

Buster stared at him. He caught on. "Oh! Go! Go!" he exclaimed.

"Merry-go-*round*!" Billy said again. They marched up to the fireplace, climbed up on the hearth. Billy slapped at the stones. He'd seen Thomas do the slapping. Be big, like Thomas. He had to hold on to the mantel, slap above it, standing on tiptoes.

Buster started hitting the stones, too. "Ouch," he said. "Come in"—murmured with a touch of pain.

Billy found the stone that could be pushed in. He hit it and felt it give. He pushed it, and the wall swung around. "Whee!"

Buster held on. It was a queer merry-go-round he was on. He knew the happiness of a merry-go-round they'd ridden sometime, and it had been fun. So this one must be fun. "Whee," he said, halfheartedly as they came around to the darkness.

"Come in!" Billy said, stepping down from the raised hearth.

"Nuh-uh," said Buster, holding on.

"Come on!" Billy commanded.

"No!" Buster said.

"Hey, you guys!" Someone spoke to them in the dark.

"Pessy!" Buster said.

"Yeah!" Pesty said. "I was just making up my mind if I would come on over. I come on back with Thomas and Great Mother. Here, take my hand, Billy. Buster, you hold on to Billy—do you want to play?"

"Yeah!" Billy said.

"Wanna go home," Buster said plaintively.

Billy took him by the hand.

"Now walk careful. It's a stairs," Pesty told them. "Take a step, one at a time."

Carefully Billy stepped down. He turned in the dark to his brother. "Take a step, Bus," he said. Buster did as he was told, but he still wanted to go home.

Then they were in the room with the one lantern glow, the perfect room from another time. Slowly the boys grew out of sorts in the evening light of wine-colored velvets and pale pink silks of the end table skirts. Buster, sensing the strangeness and smelling the ancient underground, began to cry. Hearing Buster cry made Billy whimper. Soon both boys were moaning and crying. They climbed up on the secret bed because it seemed familiar. But its sagging tick pallet did not make them feel much like marching. They got down, stumbling around, feeling lost even though Pesty was right there, watching over them. They put their heads together and bawled in earnest.

"Billy! Buster!" Pesty said softly. She knelt beside them. "Don't you know not to make noise in a cave? Could cause a cave-in. See how the dirt seeps down on the bed already? Well. Be quiet, you guys. I'm here."

"Pesty," said Billy. The boys buried their faces against her. She held them close, gently rocking them. They whimpered awhile, but they soon stopped that.

"You must've watched Mr. Thomas come through that wall. Didn't you? Well, come on. I'll show you someplace nicer to play."

The boys weren't sure. But they let Pesty lead them. She had them tightly by the wrists. They didn't mind being taken care of by her at all. Anybody bigger than themselves would do.

She took them into a low-ceilinged underground chamber, not far from the hidden room. There was some air circulation, but not much. The boys felt the closeness. Somehow it made them feel safe. There was light. They relaxed, and Pesty let go of their arms.

"This is my room, best of all," she told the boys. "Mr. Thomas don't know about this one. This one is where the orphans always stayed. See all the little beds?" There were two lanterns burning on tables next to small, low beds. The little beds were perhaps six inches off the floor on wood frames. There were grayish pallets on the frames. Each little bed had a table beside it. There were some ten beds and ten tables. Old broken things lay about on the tables. Some rags. There were a few triangles on some of the tables. Pesty had gathered most of them up and piled them across the chamber from the beds. She'd taken a box from home and filled it with the triangles. Now the box was so heavy she and her mama together couldn't move it. But a few of the triangles she had left about to play with now and then.

"See?" said Pesty. "You are the first besides me and Mama and Mr. Pluto to know about this place.. See, boys?"

They saw the low tables, the orphans' beds. Billy and Buster both had the same thought at the same moment. They said the thought at the same time, with the same words, as they often did.

"*Bears!*" they said.

Pesty laughed.

"Right!" she said. "*Two* bears instead of *three*—you two! And I'm Goldilocks. Ha-ha! Want to play with my dollies?"

There were dolls in a pile across from the beds. Over there were little chairs, small chests. The dollies were mostly rags, fallen-apart dolls that Pesty had tied back together as best she could with string and twine. She added new rags or socking when the ancient rags unraveled or fell to dust.

She gave Billy and Buster each a rag doll. She took one.

They sat with their backs to the chamber wall on a little bed, playing with the dolls. The bed was small, but so were the three of them. The pallet was musty with time, flattened and almost useless with age.

"I'll be the Indian maiden and you be the slave orphan children running for freedom—okay?" Pesty said.

"Huh?" said Buster.

"Okay," said Billy. He didn't understand, but Pesty was playing with them, and that was fun.

"Okay," said Buster.

"Now the Indian maiden is taking the orphan children through the woods to here. Mr. Drear knows she is coming. She has come lotsa times, with many children. The orphans can stay here clear through October and December and through the spring. They can rest as long as they want to in this room. They can eat and play and sleep and cry and laugh in this room." Pesty made eating motions to her dolly and began feeding Billy's and Buster's dolls. "Then the Indian maiden comes and moves them orphans a ways underground, and then they go overground along streams until they are safe."

"Safe," murmured Billy and Buster. They hugged their dolls.

"But one time the Indian maiden is followed," Pesty told them. "She has the children hide in the trees until she lures the catchers off. She starts to run. See, she's a decoy. See, a decoy is to get the bounty hunters, the slave catchers, away from the children. See, she runs real fast away. And they follow. See, that chile can run so fast! Nobody can catch her. But they do get her."

When she spoke again, Pesty's voice was somber. "They killed her. They found the children." She sighed, held her dolly tightly. "The orphans are chained in a row and taken away. Nobody knows where. And that was the last time any orphans rested in this room. 'Cept for me," she murmured. "I rest myself here all the time."

She made her doll run along the bed. She made the boys' dolls hide under her ankles, which became the trees of the woods. All the while she smiled at the boys and rocked her Indian maiden. Sometimes she made the maiden die or run to exhaustion. It was an old game with always the same ending.

"Mama says the Indian maiden was Coyote Girl," Pesty murmured. "She could outstrip anybody, any man, running. So why didn't she beat out the slave catchers? They rode their horses, that's why. They rode the Indian maiden down."

Pesty bumped the Indian maiden's head into the heads of Billy's and Buster's dolls. "Just a bunch of rags," she muttered. She threw her dolly against the opposite wall. "There goes Goldilocks!" she told the boys.

They copied her, but their throws barely cleared the foot of the bed.

Pesty leaned back and closed her eyes. Billy, Buster did the same. She pretended to go to sleep. So did the boys, mimicking her every move. They did finally sleep, at last tuckered out. Pesty dozed, too.

15

"**W**hat?" said Mr. Small as Thomas ran in. "How you doing, Thomas?"

"Papa! You'll never believe what we found!"

"Wipe your feet," his mother told him.

"Mama, we went to Mrs. Darrow's—*underground!*"

"Thomas!" said Mrs. Small.

"You did what?" Mr. Small said.

"It's true!" said Thomas. "There's a tunnel all the

way, and before you get there, there's a secret room. It has furniture I know must cost a fortune!"

"What?"

"Thomas!"

"It's true!" Thomas said desperately. "Ask Great-grandmother. Pesty took me and Great-grandmother underground—"

"She did what!"

"Thomas! You know you are to stay out of any secret passages," his mother said crossly. What he was saying hadn't sunk in. The twins' whereabouts, their safety were always on her mind. Life would be simpler when they were in school.

"It's all true," said Great-grandmother Jeffers. She was just there, right in the doorway. "Goodness!" She crept weakly over to the table.

"It's true?" Walter asked.

"Here, let me help you—my goodness!" Martha said, before Great-grandmother could answer. "You look all tired out."

"Grandmother Rhetty, it's true, what Thomas said?" Mr. Small asked.

"Aren't the boys with you?" Martha said as Great-grandmother sat down. "Did they let you come down those stairs by yourself?"

"It's true, Papa," Thomas broke in. "Everything I said is true. There's—"

"Thomas, will you shut up a minute!"—spoken harshly by his mother.

"But . . ." Thomas began.

Mrs. Small gave him her severest stare, and he held his peace a moment.

"The boys aren't with me," Great-grandmother said. "I didn't see them at all."

"Oh, they are such pistols!" Martha said. "Walter, I am so glad there is a good play school."

"Oh, did you see it?"

"Yes, and I talked to the director," Mrs. Small said. She was in a hurry to get the boys. "Both Billy and Buster seemed to like it. We can start them right away."

"It sounds good," Walter said.

"Well, we'll talk about it," she said as she left the kitchen.

"I don't get it," Thomas said. "What is wrong with everybody today?"

"What is it, Thomas?" Mr. Small asked.

"Papa, didn't you hear what I told you?"

"Now, calm down," Mr. Small said. "Start over again and take your time."

Thomas sat down beside Great-grandmother. He started over again.

Martha Small went upstairs. The rooms on either side of the upstairs hallway were silent. At the top landing she listened. She had an odd feeling of dread. Everything's going to be fine, she thought firmly.

"Billy? Buster? Come out wherever you are," she called. There was no answer as she went from room to room, opening doors when they were closed and closing doors behind her when she found them left open. The boys knew not to play in the back rooms, but when she didn't find them, she thought she'd just look anyway. "Billy? Buster? Come out now. Your papa is home. It's time for something to eat. Don't hide anymore."

Martha opened the last door and walked in, turning on the ceiling light. The bedspread was rumpled. There was pie with crust and stickiness on the carpet. The pie tin was left on the lamp table. There were streaks of dirt coming from the fireplace. She began to shiver uncontrollably. Tears sprang into her eyes. Martha sucked in her breath. She wasn't aware when she began to shout, "Walter! Walter! Help! Help! Walter, they've taken the boys!"

Thomas got to his mama first. Mr. Small was right on his heels.

"Oh, mama!" Thomas said. He saw the rumpled bed, the dirt trail on the carpet.

"They're gone!" Mrs. Small said. "The babies are gone!"

"Oh no. No . . ." Thomas cried.

"Talk, son!" his papa said sternly. "Do you have any idea where the boys are? You said there was a tunnel. Behind a wall. In this room? Quickly!"

"They must've seen Great-grandmother Jeffers and me—oh, Papa! There's a way behind that fireplace—"

"Show me! Hurry!"

"Hurry, Thomas!" Mrs. Small said.

"Get up on the hearth," Thomas told them. "Hold on to the mantel. The whole thing swings around."

They did as Thomas told them. He climbed up and pushed the stone. They began to move.

"Oh my goodness!" Mrs. Small whispered.

Slowly they turned with the wall. On the other side Thomas told them to step down. He led them down the stairs. He still had his flashlight; that was good, he thought. Soon they were in the secret room.

Walter and Martha Small stood there staring for a moment. Then Mr. Small took up the lantern that was there and held it high, so he could see the room better. Priceless furniture was the least of his thoughts. "The boys," he said to Thomas, "they're not here!"

Thomas remembered that he'd turned out the lantern his papa held; now it was back on. But he couldn't think beyond that. The underground horrified him.

"Thomas, where are they?" Mrs. Small demanded.

"I . . . don't know!" he cried.

"Think, Thomas! What is beyond this room?" Mr. Small said.

Think. Where are they? He did have an idea. "You— you go through this room, and there's a tunnel . . . to Mrs. Darrow's bedroom."

Mr. Small started through the room. Before he had gone two steps, Pesty appeared out of nowhere. "Everything's all right," she said. "Just follow me."

"Pesty! The boys . . ." Mrs. Small gasped.

"Uh-huh," Pesty said. "They're just over here." She slipped by in front of a dark rocker with a velvet cushion. She went over to the wall.

Mr. Small lifted the lantern, throwing the light up. The room was a perfect treasure, but it must wait. As if by magic, a niche in the wall appeared where there had seemed to be nothing before. It was a natural opening, an entranceway. Its position was such that it could easily be missed.

"Come on," Pesty told them.

They followed, not daring to imagine what would come next. Mr. Small held the lantern in front of him through a narrow way. Thomas was right there on his heels. Mrs. Small had slipped her hand in Thomas's.

In a moment they halted on the other side of the niche. "Papa, here's a little table!" Thomas said. There was light all around them now, more than from the one lantern his papa held. "Set the light down, Papa."

Mr. Small set his light down on a low table. He saw there were quite a few of the tables. Lanterns. The row of little beds had two sleeping occupants.

"Mama!" Thomas whispered, squeezing his mama's hand. He could have cried, he was so happy. "They're here!"

"I see them. Oh thank goodness," Mrs. Small whispered back.

"See, they're just fine," Pesty said softly. "We were playing awhile, and they went to sleep. But I was going to bring them back home when they woke up." She looked pleadingly at Mrs. Small and Thomas.

Thomas thought the evening lantern light made her face look sunburned.

"I should've brought them back to start with," she said. "I just didn't think. See, this is *my* place. I wouldn't let nothin' bother the boys here."

"What is this place?" Mr. Small asked. "You called it your place? And that other room. How long has this . . . all been here?"

"Mama's always known about the other room, and here, too," she said. "Least that's what I gather. She likes it kept neat and clean. I do that."

Thomas spoke up. "And, Papa, Mrs. Darrow is . . . I mean—" He paused, feeling sorry for Pesty, for Mrs. Darrow.

"See, my mama been sick all so many years," she said to Mr. and Mrs. Small. "Long as I can remember, her mind mostly carry on in a time long ago."

They were silent, listening to her. Finally Mr. Small said, "I see."

"Pesty, these are children's beds," Mrs. Small said. "Children slept here. . . ." Her sleeping sons stirred at the sound of her voice.

"It's the orphans' place," Pesty said. She told them about the orphans of slavery. They were the many children whose mothers and fathers had been sold away from them or had been killed. Next, she told about the doomed Indian maiden.

Thomas sat down on one of the beds. The Indian maiden wasn't a ghost, he was thinking. Mrs. Small sat down beside her little sons. They had awakened. Billy crawled into her lap. Next came Buster. It was natural for them to wake up and find their mama.

Mr. Small leaned against a table. "It's a sad tale," he said, "but one of heroism, too. I assume the Indian maiden was part Indian and part black?"

"Mama just say that Coyote Girl was a native and a relative," Pesty said.

"I understand," said Mr. Small.

"Does Macky know that the Indian maiden was such a real person? Such a—a heroine?" Thomas asked.

"He knows," she said.

So he meant to scare me out in the woods just to be mean, Thomas thought.

Mr. Small looked around the low room, aware of a vague scent from far-off times. "Does your brother know about this room," he thought to ask, "and the other room?" He nodded toward the way they had come.

Pesty shook her head no. "You can go to there and on down the tunnel and into my mama's closet and her bedroom," she said. "He don't know about that. You can't get to this orphan room unless you know to. And he don't know that either. Nobody but me and my mama and Mr. Pluto know about it. And now y'all." She looked relieved to have them know.

"So many secrets," Mrs. Small said. "Is it right for part of a family to keep secrets from the other part?" she asked gently.

"It's what my mama wants," Pesty said. "Everything to be as it was in the time of Coyote Girl—ain't that a pretty name?"

Mr. Small smiled and nodded.

Something had caught Thomas's eye. A box over there full of things. What looked like— He walked over and peered into the box of triangles. He picked up one, two and found that the triangles forced him to flex his arm muscles, they were so heavy. "Papa! There's treasure here, too. Another treasure!" And another reason to keep Macky from knowing about this place, he thought. He'd surely tell his daddy, River Lewis, to get in good with him.

"Walter, let's get the boys away from here," Mrs. Small said.

"Just a minute, Martha," Walter said. He went over to the box, picked up a triangle, and was astonished by its weight. With both hands he held it close to a lantern light. "A real one," he murmured. "Martha, this is real gold! This whole box is full of solid gold triangles!"

"I told you about them in the picture frame on Mrs. Darrow's bedroom wall," Thomas said. "I knew they had to be real." He looked at Pesty. She wouldn't meet his gaze; she looked down at her hands.

"We should leave all this alone," Mrs. Small said. She glanced around, shivering. "I don't think we should bother anything. They have kept this secret so long, Pesty and her mother. It's Mrs. Darrow's. . . ." Her voice trailed off. She stared at Pesty, at a place behind her.

Pesty turned around, grinned. There stood tall Mrs. Darrow, darker than shadow and larger than was possible. But there she was. Something about her in this . . . evening light, Thomas thought. She's not so odd in here.

They watched her as she looked over at the boys, safely on their mama's lap. Her eyes gleamed at them with tender love. "Yes, girl. Rest them! The long way home," she murmured.

They knew at once what she must be thinking.

Mr. and Mrs. Small and Thomas took their cue from Pesty. Gently now Pesty held Mrs. Darrow's hands.

Mr. Small regarded the giant of a woman whom he was seeing for the very first time. It amazed him that the thought of Pesty's mother had escaped him all this time. The Darrow men had been so dangerously on his mind he had never even considered the mother.

Mrs. Darrow's lips moved. She murmured at the

boys, her orphan children. She stirred, looking as though she would take her hands from Pesty's and go to the boys.

Quickly Pesty said, "Coyote Girl can't get through this time, Mama. So Mr. Walter and his people will take them boys." She looked over at Mr. and Mrs. Small and Thomas.

"Ahh," said Mrs. Darrow, "not my girl. They say many times she not come."

"That's right, Mama," Pesty said. "You always told me she stopped coming for the children. That's why Mr. Walter and Miz Martha taking them."

Mr. Small went cautiously to the bed. Mrs. Small touched his arm. He nodded at her, meaning yes, he meant to take the boys. He motioned to Thomas. Mrs. Darrow watched them intently, but she made no move toward them.

Thomas picked up Billy in his arms. Mr. Small took up Buster. "Now, let's move," he said quietly to Thomas.

"Mama, we're headed for the Drear house," Pesty told her mother.

"The only escape," Mrs. Darrow said. Without another word she swooped through the dark to lead, with Pesty following.

Mr. Small and Thomas, carrying the boys, and Mrs. Small made a tight circle.

"Fugitives went from here to the Drear house," Mr.

Small murmured. "Triangles gave them their direction and money they might need—"

Mrs. Small broke in. "Walter, I believe Mrs. Darrow is coming with us!"

"It's all right, Martha," he said.

"I can't help feeling frightened," she said in a hushed voice.

"I know, and it's the atmosphere down here, too," he said "But I don't think Mrs. Darrow means any harm. . . . Take the lantern there, Martha. We'll need to see our way. Only Pesty and her mother know their way in the dark."

16

"Well, hello there, Mattie," Mr. Pluto said to Mrs. Darrow. He was sitting in the kitchen, talking to Great-grandmother Jeffers.

Guess his tonic did him good! Thomas thought. Glad he and Great-grandmother got acquainted.

Pluto rose to greet Mattie Darrow as she came down the hall. "Mattie, I'm so glad you are up and around again." He folded her to him. She was as tall as he.

I'll be darn! Thomas thought. Mr. Pluto and Mrs. Darrow are *friends.*

They all entered the Drear kitchen after traveling the tunnel back home and riding the turnaround wall in the upstairs bedroom. Mr. Small and Thomas put Billy and Buster down. The boys stood there, waving at Mr. Pluto.

Mr. Pluto grinned, nodded at them, and continued. "She was Mattie Bray long before she ever married River Lewis Darrow. We are good pals! But, you know, sometimes history will get knotted up inside." He spoke softly. "You know that, don't you, Mr. Small? You are a historical man."

"Yes, I do know," Mr. Small said.

"Sometimes," Pluto went on, "history will turn itself around so, twist itself up so, it cause a mind to reel and tangle inside it." He took his arms from around Mattie and led her to one of the kitchen chairs.

Mrs. Darrow sat, clutching the sides of the chair bottom. Pesty came to stand beside her. Mattie Darrow smiled up at Pluto. "Old Skinny," she murmured.

He laughed. "She always did call me that, because my last name is Skinner. I *think* that's why!" He laughed again. "Mattie," he said, "Mother Jeffers has some soup you wouldn't believe."

Mattie glanced over at the steaming pot on the stove. "Hot pot," she said, shaking her head, "dare not."

"Good, Mama," Pesty murmured. "Keep talking."

"Oh, go ahead, dear," Great-grandmother Jeffers said to Mattie. She went over to serve the soup, taking up a bowl and filling it from the pot. "Good vegetable soup. Martha made it before she left this morning, Mrs. Darrow," she said.

"Walter's people," Mattie said, as Great-grandmother put down the soup and a spoon in front of her.

Mrs. Darrow understands a lot, Thomas thought. Being ill in the mind don't mean you can't think. Maybe it's that you think too much the wrong way, too much of the time.

Billy and Buster scrambled up on the chairs on either side of Mrs. Darrow. She stared from one to the other as though they were an amazing sight. She's seeing the orphan children, just alike, Thomas thought. Well, it can't hurt. This whole morning is just something!

Billy and Buster eyed Mrs. Darrow's soup.

"Eat, Mama," Pesty told Mattie Darrow, holding the soup spoon up to her.

"Eat, Mama," Billy and Buster said. They cocked their heads on opposite sides, staring from the soup to Mrs. Darrow, as she took the spoon.

"Eat, Mama?" they repeated, turning to Martha.

"Please, Mama?" Billy said.

Mattie Darrow chuckled with soup spoon in hand now and a full spoon of soup in her mouth. She swallowed, eyeing the boys, and turned to Mrs. Small. "Spoon the orphans!" she commanded her.

"Lord! I'm feeding them," Martha whispered. She filled Billy's and Buster's bowls from the counter. She gave them each a teaspoon and a few crackers. Mattie touched her arm. Martha jumped. Then she understood. Something more than soup. She fixed a small plate of crackers and cheese for Mrs. Darrow.

Buster leaned over Mrs. Darrow's plate. He looked up at her and carefully, not taking his eyes off her, took a piece of cheese and put it on his cracker. Then he took a second piece and put it on his brother's cracker.

All the while Mrs. Darrow watched him but made no move to stop him. Then she began feeding Pesty some of her soup. Pesty ate it hungrily. Mattie kept her eyes on the boys, observing their every move.

"Thomas, why don't you fix yourself and Pesty some soup?" his mama said.

"Okay," Thomas answered. Pesty grinned at him.

"The boys will be finished soon," Martha said. "You and Pesty can have their chairs. I need to warn them about getting into things. I'll take them upstairs."

"No!" said Buster.

"Cheese!" demanded Billy.

"Orphans, when do you leave?" Mattie Darrow hollered. The noise cut through the toddler voices of Billy and Buster. Mattie peered at them, her black, searing eyes pinning them where they were.

"They're leaving in a minute," hurriedly Mrs. Small thought to say. "Thomas, help me with them. Here's a

plate of cheese for them. Fellows, I've made hot chocolate for you to have in your room."

"I'll just go up with you-all," Great-grandmother
Jeffers said.

Martha sighed. "Good," she said.

"Mr. Pluto, it was so nice of you to drop by," Great-
grandmother said.

"Well, I expect we'll be seeing a lot of each other
around here," Pluto replied. "Good to talk to you."

"Good," Billy said. Finished eating, he got down
from the table and stood beside Great-grandmother.
Buster was right behind him.

Mrs. Darrow pushed back her chair and made to follow the boys. "Runnin' away," she said triumphantly.

"Oh, no," Martha Small whispered. "Walter? Walter!"

Mr. Pluto cleared his throat. "Mattie. They go a new
way," he said.

Startled, Mattie Darrow's hands flew to her face.

"But you and I, we'll have to go over land," Pluto
told her. He smiled at her. "We daren't all go together.
Likely we'll meet them on the road a ways."

Mattie grabbed his hand in both of hers, ready to
follow him.

"I'll take her on back now," Pluto said. He cleared
his throat. "I'm a little hoarse," he said generally.
Oddly, he wouldn't meet Mr. Small's gaze.

Mattie tugged at his arm. She turned her hooded
eyes on Pesty.

"Mama better get back before *folks* figure she ain't in the bed," Pesty said.

Meaning her brothers, Thomas thought, and her papa, Mr. "Mean" Darrow. He took his own brothers' hot chocolate and a plate of crackers upstairs, then hurried back down again.

"She's with me," Pluto was saying when he came back.

"Mama, I'll be along in a little while," Pesty said.

"Best I take her back through the house?" Pluto asked Pesty, as solemnly Walter Small watched them.

What's Papa thinking? Thomas wondered.

"Better, she slipped off out walking and stopped to see you," Pesty told Pluto, "you bring her on back home. Then no chance of somebody bein' in the bedroom and seein' her come through that closet."

"Huh," Pluto said, nodding his agreement. "I'll take her as far as the boundary of my place." He knew Mattie would not want him to run into Darrow. He wouldn't walk in on River Lewis for anything. "I'll need something to keep her warm."

Mr. Small got up. He walked around Pluto to the hallway, saying to him under his breath, "You knew about those rooms down there and the entrance to upstairs. Why didn't you tell me?"

"There was no need!" Pluto murmured. "It was Mattie's secret. . . ."

"She won't get cold," Pesty said. "Mama don't feel the cold."

Mr. Small called up the stairs to Martha for a blanket. She threw it down to him.

Pluto wrapped the blanket around Mattie. He patted her hand, said to Pesty, "She may not notice it, but she gets cold like anybody else. Mattie, let's take us a walk in the snow. We'll go for a little stroll."

"Will there be war?" she asked in her odd, wispy voice.

"Mattie, Mattie! The war *been* over!" Pluto said.

She clapped her hands. "Daylight!" she exclaimed.

They went out the kitchen door, and Mr. Small, Pesty, and Thomas listened to their footsteps crunching in the snow.

"Still cold out," Thomas said after a moment.

Mr. Small remained silent, looking at Pesty. Thomas sat next to her. His papa sat across the table from them. "Whew! Some morning!" Thomas said. But slowly he began to feel his papa's somber mood. Pesty's, too.

"I sure know what the orphan is like," she said sadly.

"It's nothing to dwell on, Pesty," Mr. Small said.

"S'what I am, though," she said, "just like them slave orphan children."

"Being an orphan is no shame, never was, and you have a family," he said.

"Some family," she said. The Darrows were the only family she'd ever known.

"Dwelling on the past," Mr. Small said gently, "it has

confused your mother's mind. We don't want that to happen to you, Pesty."

"Who cares about me?" she said, the weight of the world on her.

"I care about you," Thomas said. "You're my friend."

"We all care about you, Pesty," Mrs. Small said, coming in. "You're just like one of the family."

"Thank y'all," Pesty said. She took a deep breath and said, "My mama didn't mean nobody any harm. Did she come in upstairs? Guess she must've."

"She came down the hall and scared Great-grandmother Jeffers. But she didn't mean to," Thomas said.

"My mama been almost in bed since y'all came to the Drear house. That's why you never seen her," Pesty explained. "Then she start talking and walking."

"I see," said Mr. Small. "But why did she come here?"

"Well, wasn't never nobody here," Pesty said. "But everything change when you folks come to live here. But it won't change for Mama. She keep on walking through. That's why folks always say this house be haunted. The town kids. They probably seen Mama with her lantern going through the rooms late at night. Made her out a ghost."

"I'll be darn!" Thomas exclaimed.

"She got in here before I could stop her," Pesty said. Pesty and Thomas commenced talking about what had happened earlier in the day, when Pesty revealed the secret way into Mr. Pluto's cave.

"I am still amazed that you never told us about the rooms underground," Mr. Small said to Pesty. "They are valuable places historically."

She shrugged. "Everything was just going so well. Me and Mr. Thomas, getting along," she said. "I sure liked being around Billy and Buster and y'all." She looked shyly at Mr. and Mrs. Small.

"Well, they love being around you, and Thomas, too, Pesty," Mrs. Small said. "They consider you their big sister." Mrs. Small touched Pesty gently on the cheek. "We made everything different, didn't we, when we moved here? You've been worried to death about your mama and everything, haven't you?"

Pesty nodded, all choked up inside.

"Well, don't you worry anymore. Your mama didn't hurt anything. Now she can come visit *above*ground anytime you want to bring her over. And you know we love having *you* here. Nothing about that has changed."

Pesty looked delighted. "I thought maybe my brother Macky and Mr. Thomas might become just as close as me and Mr. Thomas."

"I don't think we ever will, if he's after treasure," Thomas said, "trying to get Mr. Pluto to tell him something. If he did come through that hole the way Pesty and I did, then some treasure was what he was after."

"We found footprints, and they looked about exactly

Macky's size," Pesty blurted to Mr. Small. She looked relieved to be telling the truth at last.

"But when your brothers and your father came to Pluto's cave," Mr. Small said, "that night months ago, when they thought Pluto was sick in the hospital and they could search their way to treasure, Macky wouldn't have any part of it."

"And so they cold-shouldered him," Pesty said. "Nobody won't talk to him all this time, except me and Mama. Won't let him hunt with them, or go into town, or work with them, or nothing. They cut him out *cold*."

"Pesty, that's terrible," Mrs. Small said.

"I'm sorry to hear that," Mr. Small said. "That kind of thing can hurt very deeply."

"Un-hum," Pesty murmured. "Guess Macky thought if he could find something, maybe gold—I bet for sure that's what got into him—he could make it up to my papa."

"He probably thought to end all of the strife in your family," Mr. Small said. "Maybe he hoped to make your mother better somehow, too."

Thomas thought to say, "Macky's a real good hunter. You can just tell by the way he gets around in the woods up there."

Mr. Small said, "Pesty, I wanted to ask you something. Does your mother know about the—" He paused and glanced toward the kitchen wall that could rise.

No telling who might be behind it, Thomas thought, following his papa's gaze.

"Does she know about the great . . . you-know-what?"

Pesty knew he meant the treasure cave. "No," she said. "Least she never mentioned about it. She sometimes slip off, to go see Mr. Pluto. He wouldn't tell her about it." She sighed. "Mr. Pluto, he don't want me to come over, go in there no more. Guess he's worried, just like you are."

"There's a lot to worry about, to consider," Mr. Small said. "I don't like all these secrets. Who knows how many more secrets there may be?" His voice shook slightly. "It's all so astounding."

"There's glass missing," Thomas said out of the blue.

"What, Thomas?" Mrs. Small said.

"Glass," Thomas repeated. "The old glass on the shelves of the you-know-what. Some of it's missing. Some broke on the cavern floor. I found the pieces, but I didn't tell Mr. Pluto."

"Somebody has gotten in!" Mr. Small exclaimed.

Thomas shook his head. "No, Papa," he said. "The broken glass was an accident. Wasn't it, Pesty?"

Sadly Thomas turned to her. "I saw the missing glass," he said to her. "Two bottles, in that first room underground. You put them there, didn't you?"

"Pesty! You didn't take rare glass from—" Mr. Small began. He stopped, seeing tears fill her eyes and spill down her cheeks.

"You did, didn't you?" Thomas said gently.

Unable to speak, Pesty nodded.

"Why did you *do* that?" Thomas said. "Why did you have to steal?"

"Thomas, that's enough," Mrs. Small said. She went over to Pesty. "Here now," she said, putting her arms around Pesty's thin shoulders. If ever a child needed a strong, sane mother, it was Pesty. Her hair hadn't been combed today. Her coat was frayed and dirty, hardly any buttons. . . .

Pesty sobbed, "I didn't mean to steal it. Didn't mean to break it! It was just—" She broke down and started to say, "It was just . . . for my . . . mama. To give her . . . something so pretty . . . to play with so she wouldn't . . . come here and run into . . . y'all."

Mr. Small shook his head.

"Poor baby," Mrs. Small whispered, hugging Pesty to her.

"Pesty, I didn't mean to make you cry," Thomas said. "Oh, I don't like having secrets, not even for a little while."

"Neither—neither do I," Pesty managed to say.

Mrs. Small gave Pesty a tissue to wipe her face.

"There's only one thing . . ." Mr. Small said, but didn't finish.

"What?" Thomas said.

His papa looked preoccupied, staring down the hall and out the door. He seemed to be seeing beyond the place where they were. "The next few days will be busy," he said. "Thomas, I want you and Pesty to go on as before. But when I tell you—Pesty, will you do something I want you to do at once?"

"Well, sure, Mr. Small," she said, wiping her eyes.

"Thomas, be ready when I need you. . . ."

"Sure! But what's going to happen?" he asked.

Mr. Small just shook his head. He was out of the kitchen, going down the hall to the parlor room, which had become his study. He closed the door behind him. After a while they heard the muffled sound of his voice on the telephone with someone.

I bet I know, Thomas thought. I bet we're going to scare the daylights out of River Lewis and all the Darrow brothers *one more time.* I *know* that's it!

Thomas, who knew how to whittle, knew how best to entertain his twin brothers, and knew something now about walking the underground, as Pesty did, was wrong this time. Wrong as he could be.

17

On Sunday life in the Drear house calmed down from the exciting day before. There were no more startling discoveries, and no one entered the house uninvited. Up early Thomas's papa shut his study door firmly behind him and talked on the telephone for a long time. He came back out for breakfast, but his expression seemed tightly closed.

Papa's not about to tell anything, Thomas thought. Thomas resolved to take Great-grandmother Jeffers to see Mr. Pluto's cave and the enormous hidden cavern. When she was still in bed, he told her, "You are just not going to believe your eyes when you see the you-know-what."

Then his mama came in, said, "Not today, Thomas. Give Grandmother Rhetty a chance! It's Sunday. It's church."

Darn! "I forgot all about it's Sunday," he said.

They took Great-grandmother Jeffers to church. The whole time there Thomas tried to be like his father, always alert, thinking and listening. My mind just wants to wander, he thought. He did enjoy hearing Pesty sing in the choir. And he pointed out Mac Darrow, playing the organ, to Great-grandmother.

But it was over at last. "You are the biggest surprise, you have the best voice I have ever heard!" Great-grandmother exclaimed to Pesty.

"Thank you," Pesty said shyly. Then she gave Mr. Small a searching look.

"That was fine singing, Pesty," he said, but he had nothing else to tell her.

What will he say when he does ask her to do something? Thomas wondered. What is it going to be about?

"Mr. Thomas, I'll see you tomorrow," Pesty said to him. She hurried on.

"I liked the way you sang," Thomas called after her as she left through a rear door. "She always sings real fine like that," he told Great-grandmother.

Mac Darrow disappeared in the time it took Pesty and Thomas to talk. Let him just fall in a hole and get lost, Thomas thought.

They ate at a restaurant out in the country at the top of a high hill. They could see the college where Mr. Small taught history. Great-grandmother said politely, "Very nice country. Pretty hills."

"Are you going to like it here, Great-grandmother?" Thomas asked.

"Oh my goodness!" she said. "You're here, aren't you? I'll like it fine!"

The next day Pesty dropped by. "Be here tomorrow right after school," Thomas told her. "We're going to take Great-grandmother to Mr. Pluto's." Pesty sat down and waited long enough for Mr. Small to come home, to see if he would say something. Mr. Small did come in at last. He saw them, greeted them, hung up his coat. He stood over Thomas a moment before going off to his study.

"Sure is busy in his head," Pesty said. "Wonder what it is he's going to ask me."

"I'm wondering if he ever will ask you something," Thomas said, "or even if he remembers he said he would."

Thomas didn't see Pesty again until Tuesday, when she came over about three-thirty.

"Hi," she said. She sat down next to him. He was having a snack.

"Hi, yourself. You got here fast," Thomas said.

"I hurried," she said.

"Won't your mama be missing you?"

"Unh-unh," Pesty said. "She wanted to walk with my daddy today, so he took her out in the fields with him."

Thomas pictured River Lewis, leading Mattie around a cornfield. He fixed Pesty a bologna and cheese sandwich, with lettuce and mayonnaise, just like his.

"Thank you," she said. "Can I have some milk?"

He got it for her. He heard Great-grandmother come out of the front parlor. The first thing this morning he had settled with her that he and Pesty would take her over to Mr. Pluto's. The day wasn't too cold, and the snow was gone.

"You'll make it just fine today, Great Mother Jeffers," Pesty said as Great-grandmother came into the kitchen.

"I'm so glad," Great-grandmother said. "I need the walk."

"It's not too cold, not too bright either," Thomas told her. "You want a sandwich before we go?"

"No, dear, I've had my lunch," she said. "Let's be on our way. I'll leave a note on the refrigerator for Martha." Mrs. Small had gone after the boys at nursery school and hadn't got back yet.

They were soon bundled up and on the outside. Great-grandmother leaned on her cane with Pesty holding her arm on one side and Thomas on the other side.

In no time, it seemed, they neared Pluto's place.

They had gone around the hill and had found an easy grade where trees gave way to an open space.

"Why, look at this!" Great-grandmother Jeffers exclaimed.

"It's a clearing," Thomas said.

Before them was a rectangular bed of flat rock. At the end of the rock was a cave. The opening was covered by heavy plank doors. "Mr. Pluto's," Pesty said. With that the plank doors opened soundlessly. And there was Pluto, big as life. His white hair and long beard were like a cushion for his green eyes, the deep brown of his face.

"Well here!" Pluto exclaimed in greeting. He sounded a little hoarse still. "Heard somebody, and guess who!"

"Yes." Great-grandmother laughed. "It's a nice walk over here."

"Come on in," Pluto said. "Bet you never been in a cave, Mother Jeffers."

"Not lately!" she said. That made Thomas laugh.

She gazed around the large underground room, thirty feet long. Its ceiling was jagged rock. And the floor was stone, a portion of which had a dark carpet. There was an armchair, a table, family pictures—they made her smile—all things one would find in a house. Great-grandmother had never seen a forge like Mr. Pluto's where he hammered iron into horseshoes and harness rings. The large bellows used to blow air for the forge fire rested on a tree stump.

"But where is the ... you-know-what-it's-called?" Great-grandmother asked.

There was a silence after which Thomas said to Pluto, "She'd like to see it," nodding his head toward one of the walls of the cave. It was a false wall.

"Well then," Pluto said, "here."

He bolted the plank doors of the cave opening. Then he walked over to the opposite wall. It was largely blank, except for a ladder leaning against it. He climbed the ladder and pulled on the rope hidden behind it. There was the grating noise of Sheetrock rubbing along the stone floor as the wall slid away.

Thomas held his breath. Great-grandmother stood looking. Mr. Pluto stepped to the side, his head slightly bowed. "Great-grandmother, see?" Thomas said, a dreamy expression on his face.

She stepped into the opening the wall had made, one hand on Pesty, one on her cane. "I lived to see this," she murmured. "Great day!"

"Dies Drear did this for us," Pluto said, "for us to save for all time."

"Let it be!" Great-grandmother said almost in a whisper.

"Let's go see," said Pluto. And they went down into the great cavern.

18

"**S**hhh! Thought I heard something,"
Thomas said. In the treasure cavern the
smallest noise seemed to hang suspended. He thought
he'd heard a sound up in Pluto's cave. Great-grandmother Jeffers had been about to read from a letter
she'd found in a century-old bondage ledger. When
she lifted the letter, pieces of it fell away from the rest.
Gently she moved the sheets until she had two facing
pages. They were part of a letter from one Pompey

Redmond, a runaway slave. The letter had been delivered to Dies Drear in 1855.

"Mr. Redmond had learned to write. You can read some of the letter, Mother Jeffers," Pluto said. "It tells a lot."

Thomas heard the sound again. They all did this time. Mr. Pluto recognized the muffled pounding. "You'd better go see," Pluto told Thomas. "Let that wall back to cover the opening. Make sure the wall ladder is in place. Don't open the plank doors to my cave, but ask who it is."

"What'll I do if it's a stranger?" Thomas had asked.

"Tell him I'm sick. Ask who, but don't let him in."

Thomas went up, did as he was told. "Who is it? What do you want?"

"It's me, Thomas, open up."

"Papa!" He unbarred the door. Mr. Small looked over his shoulder once and hurried inside.

"Did we stay too long?" Thomas asked. "I'm sorry. We were just talking. Great-grandmother Jeffers *loves* it down there. She found a letter from a slave! Papa, she and Mr. Pluto are just alike. They both just *love* it."

"Bar that door again, Thomas," his father said, grimly. He looked all around, said, "I suppose you had to bring Grandmother Jeffers here. Walking all this way—don't you realize she's no longer young?"

"But, Papa, she wanted to come," Thomas said. "Me and Pesty—"

"Pesty and I," his papa corrected.

"Pesty and I watched her every step of the way. She was fine," Thomas said.

"She could have fallen," his papa said scoldingly.

Thomas hung his head. Of course, Great-grandmother *could* have fallen. But she didn't, he thought, because we wouldn't let that happen, Pesty and me. "We would never let her fall, Papa," he finally said.

"Well, I know Grandmother Rhetty when she makes up her mind about something," his papa said. Then he changed the subject. "Show me the other way in here."

Thomas barred the plank doors. He went over to a tapestry and held it aside. There was the opening to the narrow tunnelway that led to the horse stalls. Mr. Small knew it well. "Nobody would guess it's here," he said.

They took the short walk to the stalls. Thomas showed his papa the place in the back wall where Pesty and he had entered the stall. "Now it looks like somebody's tampered with it," Thomas said.

"I see," Mr. Small answered. "So that's how they got in *if* they got in."

"I think Mr. Pluto believes they did," Thomas said. "I'm pretty sure it was Macky."

"Then let us assume that Macky got in here. That he came to worry Pluto and find out something," Mr. Small said. "But it looks like now Pluto's sealed the opening with sand and lime." He shook his head. "Nobody's coming in this way again."

"Are you sure? Not Macky?" Thomas said, resigning

himself to the fact that Mac Darrow might truly be an enemy, like his brothers.

"Not Macky or anybody else," his papa said.

They went back into the cave. Thomas climbed the ladder against the wall. He pulled the rope. The wall made its noise and swung away.

Each time Walter Small saw the enormous beauty of it all down there, he felt an urgency inside him, knotting his stomach. Each step he took down he feared the earth might tremble, bringing everything to a crumbling end. Most of all, he feared River Lewis Darrow would find his way into this awesome place. And loot it. Lord, it could happen! he thought.

They went down the natural ramp. Thomas felt the heat of the place. The steady warmth of deep underground had not changed for at least a century they knew of. He was not to raise his voice here, for any noise might set off a cave-in.

Great-grandmother Jeffers sat in a straight chair next to Mr. Pluto behind the massive desk he used. One of the slave ledgers was open on the desk. Pesty was sitting cross-legged on top of the desk. Great-grandmother smiled as Thomas and his papa came down through huge stalactites hanging from the vaulted ceiling and stalagmites rising sharply from the cavern floor. It was always splendid night deep in the underground. Mr. Pluto had lit torches all around.

Great-grandmother Jeffers began. "Dear Brother Drear," she read from Redmond's letter. "Your con-

tinuing solicitation and bid for a more secure situation
is most pleasing to this poor fugitive. . . . I am no
longer property, but am a man, and because of you.
Good citizens by the hundreds gallop out to hear
Douglass and to join the antislavery societies. But alas,
you have slavers in numbers coming up from the
southern border. I fear being forced back into cruel
Kentucky. If you beseech me to come to aid in your
labour, know that I shall. You spake darkly of a great
underground. What might be your meaning? What
plan, Brother Dies? Forgive this wretched soul and its
folly of weakness . . . I dread journeying the black for-
ests that lie between me and thee. . . ."

Mr. Small paced back and forth in front of the desk.
Great-grandmother Jeffers stopped reading. Her eyes
shone with pride in the fugitive, Redmond.

"Papa, wasn't the great underground he mentioned
this treasure place?"

"So it would seem, Thomas," Mr. Small spoke softly.

"All this time Pompey Redmond has been waiting to
tell us something," Great-grandmother said with feeling. "Would've been something to help him along!"

"Would've indeed," Mr. Pluto said. "Not hard to see
how Mattie Darrow came to be the way she is. Living
the underground the way she does. Ah, the meanings
of the word—'underground'!"

Mr. Small stopped his pacing. He turned to Pesty,
sitting on the desk. "The time has come," he told her.
He looked at Pluto. Something in the look made Pluto

get up. The dark throw flowed and settled around him like a shroud. "The time has come," Mr. Small repeated to Pluto.

"No." Pluto's mouth shaped the word soundlessly.

"Thomas, we have to go now," Mr. Small said. His hand went briskly through his hair. "Pesty, you, too. Let's go."

Quickly Pesty got down and stood next to Thomas. "Grandmother Rhetty," his papa said, "Martha's back with the boys. We saw your note. I'll drive the car over as far as I can, and you won't have to walk the whole distance."

"I'll stay right here, then, until you return," she said, at Pluto's side.

Pluto's eyes glinted hard at Mr. Small. "You think I'm too old," he said. His woolen throw spread over his arms like raven wings. "I can't carry Mother Jeffers home in my buggy? You think I can't protect someone . . . this—"

"A buggy ride!" Great-grandmother exclaimed. "Oh, I'd love that. I haven't had a buggy ride in thirty years!"

"Well, have one now then," Mr. Small said. And to Pluto: "I meant no offense. I know how well you handle a horse-drawn buggy. I just thought . . ."

"You just thought to tell everybody what to do," Pluto said quietly, sadly.

"Mr. Pluto, I'm doing the best I know how," Mr.

Small said shakily. "I must see you tonight. I'll be back."

Pluto looked surprised. He studied Mr. Small for a moment but said nothing.

"Come on, children, we've things to take care of," Walter Small said. Thomas and Pesty went out with him. Pesty glanced shyly back at Pluto and Great-grandmother and waved.

"Bye," Thomas said to them.

They could hear Pluto following. He would lock the doors of his cave behind them. Great-grandmother was reading again: "The Philadelphia Vigilance Committee heeds your call. Mr. Purvis gave to me food and clothing and a place to rest at his estate. I met more abolitionists from everywhere."

Outside Pesty, Thomas, and his father walked in silence for a time, toward the Drear house. Mr. Small was deep in thought. "Papa, what is it?" Thomas said.

"It's just the time," his papa said. "It's a good and bad time."

"What do you mean, Papa?"

"I mean, we've kept the great cavern secret for so long. I've been inventorying everything all these months, to give a listing of the treasure to the foundation that owns the house and the hill. That's what I told myself I was doing." He laughed. "Well, I never gave them a list of anything. I kept it all to myself. Still a secret. And I as much as promised Mr. Pluto that I would not tell the foundation anything as long as he lived." He sighed. "Well, I had no right to promise such a thing! And now what has to be done makes me very sad—"

"What's that?" Pesty asked. "What's it that has to be done?"

Mr. Small stared down at the ground for a long moment before he said, "Well, it's a plan worth trying. Pesty, your share of it has two parts. The first thing in the morning I want you to get your mother out of the house and into our house without anyone else knowing. Can you do that?"

"Sure!" she said. "We can go the tunnelway, and if it's morning, everybody just think Mama is taken to bed or is sleeping late."

"And Pesty, after bringing your mother, will you go back and do something else important?" Mr. Small said.

"What's that?" she asked.

He told her, speaking just above a whisper. Thomas listened. His eyes grew wide, startled, as he heard it all. Looking all around, Mr. Small made sure that only the three of them could hear. "Timing is everything," he told them. "Pesty, you must have your mother in our house by eight o'clock tomorrow morning."

"Eight o'clock," she said. "She don't sleep long these times. I can do it. We'll be out in the tunnel by eight anyway."

"No, in the house at eight," Mr. Small said firmly.

"And no later than eight-ten, you hear? Because the last part comes at nine. You remember?"

"Yes," she said, "I—I just hope I don't get in worse with . . ." She wouldn't name her papa, River Lewis, but that was whom she was thinking about.

Mr. Small knew it. "Let's hope that everything happens just the right way, so there is no time for *folks* to think about how and why it's happening.

"Timing. Timing!" he continued. "Once and for all. There's no other way. . . . The timing must be perfect."

"But I don't understand, the part about—" Thomas began.

Mr. Small stopped him. "I've said all that needs to be said for now. Wait until tomorrow. Seeing is believing, Thomas, and this you have to see."

Supposing something goes wrong? Thomas was thinking. Supposing the Darrow men . . . and Macky— he didn't want to think what would happen if things went wrong.

Although she had misgivings, Pesty trusted Mr. Small. "Wish things wouldn't always change," she said. "Then again I wish they would."

"Me, too, Pesty," Mr. Small said.

Everything's up in the air. What if Pesty gets into trouble? Thomas was thinking. What if Pluto gets mad at Papa, or Mrs. Darrow can't be moved? And River Lewis, what if . . . ? The what-ifs made his head spin.

19

Thomas woke up early and dressed quickly. He paused long enough to think: Good luck, Pesty! Next, he put her out of his mind while he made sure his papa was still confident about everything, that Great-grandmother was ready. He guessed that was his part of the plan to do. Papa sure didn't give me a lot to work out in perfect timing, he thought.

He was right about what Pesty would be doing. She

and Macky were up first, while it was dark out. Next, her daddy was up, and her older brothers, Wilbur, Russell, and River Ross. Her mama might stay awake all night. Or she might sleep and wake up a million times. Or like these days, she would wake up peacefully and want to get dressed to go walking. Pesty had a time with her. Today she would need to keep her mama quiet for more than an hour. She'd told Mr. Small she could do it. Mr. Thomas had heard her say so.

Pesty awoke at ten minutes past six. Not bad, she thought. The house was cold. She blew her breath; it was like white mist on the air. Wonder how many breaths it take to warm this room? She got up and got dressed. Shivering, she put on boots that were the warmest shoes she had. Remember boots for Mama. And her coat, too. Keep her good and warm.

In the kitchen she started the fire in the big old cookstove. She washed up in the cold water pumped into the sink from the well and dried her face and hands. By that time there was a roaring fire in the stove. She put the water kettle on to boil. When the flames settled down, she added pieces of wood and soft coal from the bucket next to the stove. Now I wash my hands *again!* She always did that when she lit the fire.

She put peanut butter and jelly on the toast, boiled eggs and instant coffee. She had it all on a tray when Macky came in. "Morning. Mama hungry this morning," she told him, forcing herself to smile.

"What you been doing?" he asked her. It was his

chance to talk to her with no one else around. "You stay over there at that house all the time. What have you been up to?"

She couldn't get over how fast he'd got on her trail. "I was over to Mr. Pluto's, too, yesterday," she said pleasantly. "And Mr. Thomas and me play with the little guys some, over his house. They go to school, too. We hang out with Great Mother Jeffers. She a lot of fun, and we took her to Mr. Pluto's." All the time she spoke, she was moving out of the kitchen, away from him. Macky stood there, rocking on his heels. Looking angry and defeated, he watched her go.

Pesty ran into her daddy. He was looking in on Mattie. He had closed the door, so Pesty knocked. River Lewis Darrow opened the door. "Morning, Daddy," she said as softly as she could. He blocked her view, and she couldn't see if her mama was awake.

River Lewis eyed her and stepped to one side so she could pass through with the tray. He nodded curtly, but he did not speak to her. It made her feel bad, never to have her daddy say hardly a word to her.

Mattie was sitting up in bed. River Lewis went back to sit down in the chair. Pesty remembered that Great Mother Jeffers had sat just there.

Mama seem not to mind Great Mother, Pesty thought. She looking pleasant this morning, too. "Morning, Mama," she said. "How you feeling today?"

Mattie laughed suddenly. "I bent my back down the

road," she said happily. "I squirreled the tree and gave a hoot."

Pesty sighed. "Okay, Mama, I got some food for you and me. Eggs and toast—how 'bout that?"

"I treed a squirrel, that was my dream," Mattie said. "But going down the road backward—I don't know."

Pesty grinned, delighted. When her mama could figure out her own words, she was doing better than ever.

Pesty took part of the food and put it on the night table. Then she took the tray and handed it over to her daddy.

River put the cup of coffee in Mattie's hand. "Now take a good, long drink," he said. "This room is coolish. I'll bring in a heater if you want."

"No, thank you," Mattie said. Her voice sounded less disconnected this morning, thought Pesty. She's doing better, but it won't last.

Pesty ate some of the food. River Lewis and Mattie chatted after a fashion, as Mattie ate her breakfast. So did Pesty and her mama chat. But River and Pesty had few words spoken between them. She hoped he would talk to her. All the time she was careful not to mention any of the Smalls.

Her older brothers came in to speak for a moment to their mother. Big, bungling men. The room seemed crowded with them in it. They shuffled their feet back and forth. They said they would see her later, and they went out. Macky came in, joined his father and Pesty around the bed.

"Morning, Mama. Daddy," he said.

"Ah, Macky," his mama answered.

River Lewis said nothing. It wasn't a minute before he got up and walked out of the room. Some of Mattie's pleasant mood went with him. She frowned at Macky. Then she seemed to forget there was any change or that River Lewis had gone, had ignored his youngest son for one more day.

Mattie patted the coverlet, and Macky came over to sit down.

"It's chilly today, Mama," he said. He put his head down on her pillow next to her, with his face facing away from her. She reached around and held his head in the crook of her arm.

Macky always was her favorite, Pesty thought, watching. She didn't mind that. He was her mama's own last child. She was her mama's own first and last orphan girl. Each has a place. I never got in the way of any child's place.

"I'm going to stay with you, Mama," Macky said. "Stay here the whole day."

"*No!*" Pesty hollered inside. Often Macky said he would stay the whole day. You know he's not staying, she thought. Don't let anything go wrong. What time it is? Is it time? Couldn't be more than seven o'clock. Time left, but I got to get her up and going.

Mattie Darrow had been watching Pesty over Macky's head. She cradled her youngest son. Big old boy, Pesty thought.

Macky had his eyes closed and did not see Pesty's expression. But Mattie did. She stared at her orphan child, whom she kept safe in her house and hoped never to send along the underground road.

"Mama, didn't you say you wanted some wild meat?" Pesty said. "Didn't you, Mama?" She dared give her mama a clue that wouldn't hurt anything, to say something that would help get rid of Macky. Her mama did love wild meat so.

"Squirrel? Squirrel?" her mama murmured.

Macky lifted his head. "Mama, you want me to hunt you squirrel? Haven't had some squirrel in a long kind of time," he said. "Been eating too much house meat anyhow." Meat bought in the stores was called house meat.

"Cut it up and parboil it. Squirrel," Mattie said into Macky's hair.

"You got to shoot him first," he said. "Then you ring his hind legs at his feet. You have to cut around that tail base. Put him on his back."

"Put your foot on his tail," Mattie said, and cackled loudly.

"Grab him by his back legs," Pesty added.

Macky gave her a dirty look. "This between my mama and me," he said.

"Soak him," Mattie said. "We always soak him."

"Who, we?" Macky asked. But she was silent on the subject.

"She means when she was a girl," Pesty said.

"How you know she means that?"

"I always know what she means," Pesty said. "She's my mama, too."

"No, she's not." He had his eyes closed again.

Mattie's chin rested in his hair. She stared at Pesty.

Pesty felt sick at heart. Things change, she thought, and swallowed away the lump in her throat.

"I got to go," Macky said to Mattie. He got up.

"Bushy tail," Mattie said, smiling. She shielded her eyes, as if looking into the sun.

"I'll get you maybe some squirrel," he said. "I'll go see what I can find in the woods today. You want this?" He held up the toast she hadn't touched. She took it, took two bites, gave it back to him. He wolfed it down, going out the door.

Nobody saying goodbye, Pesty thought. She felt so bad today. Living in this house with nobody to talk to most of the time. Now Macky didn't want her around.

Her papa drank his coffee in the kitchen. So did her older brothers. Macky waited in his room. When they were gone, he went in and had some milk and cookies. He got his gun from the high gun shelf in the pantry. And he left.

Everybody hates me, Pesty thought. She stood just inside her mama's bedroom at the doorway, looking out. She saw everybody leave. Then she closed the door and turned the skeleton key in the lock.

"Mama, get your clothes on! We got to get going in the tunnel."

Mattie Darrow was out of bed, suddenly rushing, tearing up the room.

"Mama, shhhh. Slow down! Here. Sit. I'll get your clothes and your coat, and your boots, too. You want to go to the bathroom? Okay, Mama. And you wish to wash up, too. I'll comb your hair when you are finished. It was seven-fifteen when Daddy left. Now it's some later, so please, Mama, hurry! Oh, it's going to be a big day, I bet!"

It was just after eight when Mattie and Pesty swung around into the bedroom upstairs in the house of Dies Drear. Thomas and Mr. Small and Great-grandmother Jeffers were there waiting. "We'll go downstairs to the kitchen," Great-grandmother said, after greeting Pesty and her mama. She took Mattie Darrow ever so gently by her arm. Mattie made no resistance.

They all went downstairs. Pesty hung back with Mr. Small and Thomas.

"They all of them are out the house," she told them.

"Can you get them on time?" asked Mr. Small.

"Sure. They're just out doing chores."

"Macky, too?" asked Thomas.

"No. He's hunting. Squirrel, 'cause Mama wants it. But I can get him."

"It would be good if you did," Mr. Small said. "But get your father and the others. You know what to do. I'm counting on you."

"I know it," she murmured. She smiled shyly at Thomas.

He smiled back at her. "It's going to come out great," Thomas said.

"I know it," she said. But she was thinking: Am I right to do this?

They stood at the bottom of the stairs. "Mama won't be any trouble, long as Great Mother Jeffers is there," she told Mr. Small. "She likes Great Mother Jeffers. She likes Thomas, too." She and Thomas grinned at each other. "Have the little fellows gone off to school yet?"

"Not yet," said Thomas.

"Well, she'll sure like seeing them best of all."

"Pesty, I want you to know that we all think you are just wonderful," Mr. Small told her.

"You do?" she said.

"Uh-huh," he said. "You are smart and very brave, and we thank you now for everything. I promise you, everything is going to work out, you'll see." But he hated seeing the sadness in her eyes.

"I'm going then," she said.

"We'll see you in a short while," he said. "Remember, the timing is everything. Don't tell before nine o'clock. Then get them moving."

"I know," she said. "See you." And she left, wanting only to be in the Drear kitchen, where it was warm and smelled so good. She went out the door and jumped off the front porch. She started her trot home.

20

Pesty stopped trotting to study the wooded hilltop. She gave a yell, "Mah-Kay! Mah-Kay!," calling her brother. She could hear her voice a long way around, coming back to her. There, she thought, Macky better hear *that*! But for good measure she called out again: "Mah-kay! Mah-kay!"

She could trot forever. But it wasn't far now. She jogged on along the bottom of the rise on Drear lands clear to the east toward her own family land. It was her mama's father's land. They had twelve acres sandwiched between Drear and Carr lands. Her daddy grew low-grade corn for silage. Now it was winter and not much to do. Her daddy did a lot of walking the countryside.

Still looking for treasure, and it's right under his nose. Why does he have to have riches? she wondered. He'd kill me if he knew that all this time— She dared not think about it.

Pesty slammed inside the house just to make noise. There was no one there. She made her mama's bed. She never bothered to make her own or anyone else's. The clock said seven minutes to nine. Not long now. She went into her mama's bedroom and lay on the bed, closed her eyes. All was silence around her.

"I'm just a kid," she whispered into the pillow, feeling sorry for herself. Am I wrong to help Mr. Thomas's papa? What is going to happen?

She heard a gun go off a long ways off. Her eyes flew open; she saw it was nearly time. She got up, giving herself a minute to leave the house, to trot around to the fields. Her daddy would be nearby. What if he's not? What if he's gone off to town? She had a moment of panic and screamed at the top of her lungs. "Daddy! Daddy! Daddy, hurry, something's happened!" she hollered. She knew it must be nine o'clock. "Dad-dy!"

Where there had been no one, River Lewis Darrow

was suddenly there. He was climbing over a fence near Pesty. "Daddy!" she yelled, running to him.

He looked slightly to one side of her when he spoke. "Mattie all right?" he said, alarmed by her hollering.

"Daddy! Come quick. Everybody over Mr. Pluto's. Say there's been a great discovery." Pesty stood there panting.

River Lewis stopped still. He didn't move a muscle, and he looked as if he had been struck dumb. His boys, Wilbur and Russell and River Ross, came up.

"What is it, Daddy?" River Ross asked. River Lewis waved him quiet.

"Say again? Slowly," he finally said to Pesty.

Pesty took a deep breath and started over. "Daddy, all them Smalls, over to Mr. Pluto's. Everybody yelling. Mr. Small says to Mr. Thomas, 'Thomas, this is a great discovery.' Mr. Thomas, jumping up and down. Mr. Pluto, he had a handful of *gold*. Just lumps and lumps of *gold*. He given it to Mama!"

"Wh-what?" River Lewis stammered. "Mattie, over there? Gold?"

"She like to walk, so I walk her on over to Mr. Pluto's 'cause she's his friend," Pesty said, "and she's right in the middle of some great discovery."

Before Pesty had finished, River Lewis was moving by her; the older sons were right with him. Then River Lewis was nearly running, and his sons were still with

him. Pesty trotted at the rear. Wasn't any use talking
more about it. She had done her part.

They were nearly at Pluto's. They had skirted Carr
property and were passing by the woods when Macky
walked out of the trees. He had his gun over his arm
and pointing toward the ground. There was something
still in a burlap sack slung over his shoulder. "What's
going on?" he called, trotting down to catch up with
Pesty. "Were you yelling my name?

"Well, sure," Pesty said. "You catch anything?"

"Sure, some squirrel," he said. "But what did you
want? Where's everybody going?"

River Lewis and the older sons hadn't stopped. They
paid no attention to Macky as usual. "Just come on,"
Pesty said, trotting again. "We have to get over to Mr.
Pluto's for the great discovery."

"The what?" he said, carefully setting his gun and
the sack down. He would pick them up later.

"Mr. Small says to his son, Mr. Thomas, 'Thomas,
this is a great discovery,'" Pesty explained. "And Mr.
Thomas, a jumping bean. His mama there, too. She
already taken the twins to school and come back. And
Great Mother Jeffers say, 'Praise heaven and earth!'
And Mr. Pluto, he have a handful of gold. He give it to
Mama!"

"He what?" Macky said.

"Just come on, Macky, and you'll see!" Pesty said.

She and Macky went, following River Lewis and the
older brothers, who were truly hurrying now. When

they reached the clearing before the cave, the men stopped in their tracks.

"Careful," River Lewis whispered. He was remembering the last time they thought to enter Pluto's cave. Then the Smalls with Pluto and his son, Mayhew, had played the awful trick on them, scaring River Lewis and his boys to death. He half suspected that little Pesty had been in on it, although he was never able to prove it. Pretending slave ghosts and Dies Drear ghost had come back to haunt the place and everything. Made him look like a fool when folks found out his boys had run in fear. He'd barely lived it down. Now here he and his sons were back again. And were they to be made fools of twice?

"Daddy, them doors to the cave is open," said River Ross.

"I can see that," River Lewis said. "Do you think I'm blind?"

"No, Daddy," River Ross said.

River Lewis skirted the clearing. He intended to turn and swagger off at the slightest movement inside. But there was nothing, no sound or anything. The doors to the cave were open partway, but not enough so they could see inside.

Pesty held her breath as River Lewis reached the door. He stood for a second. Then he roughly pushed the plank doors all the way open. Not bothering to knock, he walked on in. After all, his wife must still be inside. His older sons came on behind him. Then Pesty and Macky came in.

Within, Pluto's cave was the way it always was after breakfast. The bed was neatly made. But the forge and firepot, the bellows and anvil were cold and still today. The wood roof doors in the rock ceiling were open to the cold and light. Pesty could see a piece of sky surrounded by bare limbs of trees.

The secret wall across the cave from them had been made to slide away.

"Look!" whispered River Lewis. "Didn't know that opening was there!"

"Daddy . . ." Wilbur said.

"Shut up!" River Lewis whispered loudly. Wilbur clamped his mouth shut.

Cautiously River Lewis moved up to the wall opening.

When he stands right in front of it, he will see, Pesty thought. Her heart leaped in her chest. Glad I won't have to keep it a secret no more.

River Lewis stood at the opening, as still and dark as shadow. He was looking down. They all came up behind him, stood on either side. The opening was that wide. They had to look down into the underground cavern. Darrow men stood there, thoughts rushing so. Pesty, seeing Thomas inside looking up, could almost hear her daddy thinking: This wealth, right underfoot. Forever here. All this time.

They all were down there: Smalls and Pluto, Pluto's

son, Mayhew Skinner. He was an actor. See, Pesty? Thomas was thinking. We got hold of Mayhew, too, so Mr. Pluto would feel better about it all.

Mayhew stood coolly, smiling up at the Darrows. Pesty was glad to see him. He was her friend and always nice to her. She'd seen him on television in a commercial once. She didn't get to see him in real life so often.

Her mama was there with Mr. Pluto on one side of her and Great Mother Jeffers on the other. Next in line were Mr. and Miz Small.

The Darrow men, River Lewis and the boys, including Macky, who'd never known the treasure existed, walked down the ramp like sleepwalkers. They were staring at the stalactites as if they'd dreamed them. They avoided touching the monstrous things. Stalagmites rose from the floor, seeming to guard what had to be one of the greatest discoveries ever uncovered: the great cavern, the stupendous treasure-house of Dies Eddington Drear.

River Lewis Darrow moved along as in a trance. His sons stumbled behind him, jostling one another and tripping over their own feet. He kept slapping back at them weakly. But none of them, not even Macky, said a word. Without even thinking about it, they all knew that they must not make loud noise in a cave this size.

They stared dumbly at everything. Mr. Pluto stood beside the Renaissance desk that commanded the approach to the cavern. He rested one hand on the polished top. His brown woolen throw over his shoulders made him look like a king: King Pluto of the Drear Underground.

The Darrows had reached a rampart arch in the downslope of the ramp. Here they could stand almost level. And here they paused to gape.

The barrel-shaped cavern ceiling rolled up and up over them. It was half a football field long. High up, on all sides, hung Persian carpets and rich tapestries. Their colors glowed in the flame light of Mr. Pluto's torches, grouped in the center. On the cavern floor between the hangings were whole painted canoes and finely crafted totem poles. Tens upon tens of bureaus and breakfronts, inlaid with delicate woods, had drawers packed with small treasures. There were scores of barrels bursting with silken and embroidered materials set in rows between canoes and poles. Riches spilled from kegs and crates—gold coins and gold watches, pearls and other jewelry that sparkled and nearly blinded their eyes. The astonishing hoard went on and on, practically as far as the eye could see.

Thomas thought he saw light and mist in Darrow's eyes as River Lewis came closer. But Darrow blinked again twice, and the glinting was gone.

Through the corridors of grandeur and wealth walked several strangers. There was the whir and click of a camera, a flash of light. A man and woman came up the ramp toward the Darrows. The man had been taking photographs of the cavern wealth for half an hour. Now he was ready to take shots of these new people making their way down. The Darrow men were tall, light-skinned, and rather sinister-looking. In their astonishment they made quite a picture.

"You're Mr. River Lewis Darrow?" the woman said, keeping her voice down. Everybody looked up at Darrow. "I'm a reporter, Nancy Enders, from the Springville *Star*. Pleased to meet you, Mr. Darrow." The woman extended her palm. River Lewis shook her hand mechanically up and down twice.

"This is my photographer, Jeremy Johns," she said. "Could you tell us what you think about your wife's helping to discover this cavern?" She pushed a key of her tape recorder and held the recorder out toward River Lewis.

Darrow stared at the woman in disbelief. It was then that Mr. Small spoke quickly before River Lewis had time to think.

"Morning, Mr. Darrow," he said pleasantly, as though he greeted Darrow every day. He moved closer as Darrow took a step back in surprise at the greeting.

"There are people from the area newspaper here," Walter Small said. "I expect there will be more later. They'll all want to talk to you. And the folks over there are the people who run the foundation that owns Drear property. They are looking over all the treasure."

Right on that Mr. Pluto spoke, came forward with Mattie, his hand at her elbow. The gold she had held in her hands was now magically on the grand desk. There sparkled a discreet pile of nuggets, pretty and golden as you please.

"Wouldn't you know it would happen like this?" Pluto was saying, nearly in a whisper. He knew it was what he wouldn't say, the words he left out, that would make his point to Darrow. "And like nobody, Mattie come in, and stare at that wall of my cave. I stare at that wall every day. She look at me; I look at her. Something about that wall we see different. Wouldn't you know it would happen like that? So unexpected, out of the blue! That wall move, and . . . all this here."

There. He said his part. It was only part little white lie or even part huge lie. There were places left out between the words he'd said. It didn't matter that later Darrow might realize again what he always knew: that it would take considerable time to discover a great treasure. For now it was over. All of it gone, the enormous cavern, all taken from him, Pluto, and Darrow, too, for that matter. Pluto wouldn't protest, wouldn't make a fuss over what Mr. Small had done. How could he? I'm an old man, Pluto thought. I've no real right to the property, the treasure-house.

Mr. Small had convinced him that a cave-in could happen, that the great cavern belonged truly to—what had Small called it?—"posterity," the future of them all.

Mayhew will take care of me. He's my own son,

doing well for himself now. But I've never had to depend on someone. Never!

Tall and lean, Mayhew Skinner, Mr. Pluto's son, moved to the other side of his father from Mattie and put his arm around him. He saw the gloom spread over Pluto's face. "Hey, it's okay, don't worry," he murmured to his father. Mayhew had known Darrows all his life. Even when he had moved away from Drear land and the town, he'd never forgotten them and had kept tabs on them. Mattie Darrow had always been strange, always out of place. But he'd thought kindly of her because his father had cared about her welfare and what she cared about—keeping safe the underground. Now Mayhew tightened his hand on his father's shoulder as a comfort. There was a grim, faint smile on his lips. His eyes glinted hard yet amused at River Lewis and his "boys"—grown men, all.

Thomas watched the scene unfold, transfixed by the sight of so many people, friend and foe and even strangers. The daring of his father's plan was just so fantastic. It all was happening the way it was supposed to happen.

Thomas went up the ramp a few feet, and for the first time he wasn't nervous around Darrows. He walked around the Darrow men to stand next to Pesty, right by Macky. He folded his arms and held his head high.

"It's the only way," he remembered his papa's telling

Mayhew last night. "We bring Darrow *inside* the cavern. Up *front* where everybody can see him."

"But why?" Mayhew demanded to know.

"Because"—Thomas had said; his papa's plan made good sense to him—"the best place to keep a secret safe is to bring it and the enemy of it out in the open. That way there can't be harm in either of them ever again."

"Mr. Darrow," the reporter was saying, "can we get a picture of you and your wife . . . and Pluto—er, Mr. Skinner?" She had not waited for Darrow to answer her first question. Seeing that he was so stunned by all the people and commotion, the great cavern itself, she had asked this next question of him. She smiled and politely pulled Mr. Pluto with Mattie Darrow over to River Lewis. She placed them so Mattie stood between Pluto and Darrow. Darrow was like a pillar of stone that couldn't be moved. Mayhew stood close by, not trusting Darrow near his father.

Mattie stared into River Lewis's face. "You stand on my side," she told him. He looked at her, confused but realizing why she was there. His face worked in dismay. His eyes had blackened in anger and grief as he surveyed what he'd lost. His own wife had helped in the great discovery. More's the pity!

Great balls afire! he raged inside. Here was what he'd longed for most of his life, and his father before him, and *his* before *him*. His poor Mattie was in on it, too! And *they* taken it from me. *They!*

Wasn't going to be his atall!

It ain't fair! Inside, River Lewis moaned in sorrow-
ing anger. Damn your soul, Walter Small, you and
your *do-right!*

Cameras flashed, clicked. The reporter wouldn't go
away. She had tried to interview Mattie and had found
her impossible. Now she really had to have answers to
a few things more from the husband, at least, to round
out her story. All these people, living half in the light
and out.

"What do you think you and your wife will do with
her part of the reward?" she asked. "The foundation
states it is considering seriously giving a reward to the
discoverers of the treasure."

Darrow tried to hide his shock at the news. "Have to
think about that," he mumbled, fidgeting there in the
limelight. But it was clear from the gleam in his eyes
that a reward of money had caught his attention.

A moment later Mr. Small asked everyone to leave
the cavern. "There's more to be seen," he announced
in a quiet voice to everyone. He started up the ramp
past Darrows, leading the way. He talked softly as he
went, like a museum guide with a sore throat, Thomas
thought. "Granted, the next discovery is not as grand
and rich as this formidable place," he continued. "Yet
its history is very significant all the same." He hoped
that no one would notice he'd not said who had made
the next discovery. No need to get Mattie involved
again. "There's a story of an Indian maiden in these

parts"—he hurried on—"and the tale is connected to another natural underground area."

"Wish he wouldn't go do that," Pesty said, watching her mama. Mrs. Darrow's face was like a storm. She had heard what Mr. Small had said about the Indian maiden. She turned hard, slashing eyes on him.

"Now, Mattie," Mr. Pluto said, "it will be all right. Let Mr. Small alone."

"She's going to be all right," Pluto said to Mr. Small. "You can go ahead."

Her mama's hands were shaking, Pesty saw. "Wish he wouldn't tell," she said. Thomas heard her. His papa began telling the Indian maiden tale.

"He has to tell it, Pesty," he whispered. "The orphans' place is real . . . history. The other room down there is, too. There can't be secrets now."

"But what about my mama?" she said in anguish.

Thomas hadn't thought about how much the underground rooms had become Mattie Darrow's life. He would have to think about it.

Outside in the air, Pesty took hold of her mama's hand. "It's all right, Mama," she said. Mattie looked all around, patted River Lewis on his cheek. It was such a loving touch, Thomas thought. And then Pesty led her away.

"Mattie," River Lewis called. He stood near the plank doors of Pluto's cave. His big sons were right on his heels. Macky was the last to step outside.

"Taking her home," Pesty called to River Lewis.

"Hello!" Mattie called to him, saying goodbye.

River Lewis stared after Pesty and Mattie. He wouldn't leave, not now.

But Macky would. Macky walked away toward his mama and his sister. He kept his head down.

That's that, Thomas thought. Pesty and Macky, Mrs. Darrow, they don't care anything about treasure. He stood around at the side of Pluto's cave. There were two cars waiting on the far side of the clearing. The foundation people and Mr. Pluto now gathered, going in one car, careful of trees. Then the newspaper folks went by themselves, following the first car. The rest of them—Darrows, Mayhew Skinner, Thomas, and his papa—went quickly on foot toward the Drear house. It wasn't far, and they would be only a few minutes behind the automobiles.

Mr. Small walked briskly alone. After him, Thomas walked beside Mayhew. River Lewis and his boys brought up the rear. It was sure different having Darrows around all of a sudden, Thomas thought. Before, River Lewis and his sons were the last people I'd want to see, except for Macky. Still are, too, I guess.

He didn't like their cold, calculating silence. Didn't like taking them onto Drear lands, taking them home. Taking them into our house.

Darrows, who early on had crept through the house to scare his family away. They had come, not like Mattie, who couldn't help herself from wandering, but sneakily, like thieves in the night.

The final part of his papa's plan was to take the Darrows and the others through the hidden places of the house. Show them everything. So that all would be known and seen and done at last.

21

They were snow-covered mounds behind the shed. Their only movement was when they stuck out their tongues to taste the snowflakes and when their snow-filled eyelashes blinked. Pesty had brought along the blanket Mr. Small had lent Mattie and snuggled inside it.

It was Sunday. Maybe his folks and everybody would go to church, but Thomas didn't think so. Not with all that had happened to them since Wednesday. It was the fourth day after what became known to him and his family and Pesty as THE EVENT, "in capital letters," his mama had said. And so *it*, THE EVENT, still waved banner-high in Thomas's thoughts. Because of *it*, they all had become "some famous," as Great-grandmother Jeffers put it.

Thursday evening the headline in the local Springville *Star* had been: DREAR PROPERTY YIELDS VAST TREASURE—AN UNDERGROUND CAVERN OF SPLENDOR IS UNCOVERED. A FURNISHED NINETEENTH-CENTURY UNDERGROUND ROOM AND SLAVE ORPHANS' SLEEPING QUARTERS UNDISTURBED FOR OVER A CENTURY. A long account of the THE EVENT followed.

Pesty was happy to be famous but sad that everything had changed so. She worried about what her mama might do when she discovered her underground sitting room was going to be crawling with people of the foundation. And what would Mr. Pluto do without the great cavern? Do is already done, she thought, do, done, and gone. She moved, shedding snow. "If this keeps up, it's going to pack good when it turns colder," she said.

"Then, tomorrow, we'll make some snowpeople," Thomas told her.

To their amazement, they were in the Thursday evening paper on the third page, where the account ended. On the front page was a picture of Pluto, Mattie, and River Lewis, with the cavern to their backs. River Lewis looked furious and stunned both at the same time. The photograph appeared more than once in forty-eight hours and in more than one paper. The photo on the third page showed Martha and Walter Small and Great-grandmother Jeffers. Great-grandmother was holding a slave ledger up for everyone to see. In the foreground of the picture knelt Thomas and Pesty. They were smiling. Held between them was a cast-iron pot full of gold. Mr. Pluto had rummaged around until he found something to put the gold in that would show it off. "Pot of Gold at the End of the Rainbow," the paper said.

Thomas got his picture taken two more times. In one of them he was sitting on an orphan's bed, with the whole cave room viewed behind him, lit by flashbulbs. In the other he held up one of the gold triangles from the box of them.

The identity of each person was given under every picture and separate from the news story. The articles all said that Mr. Pluto and Mattie Darrow were the discoverers.

"Still more secrets, though," Thomas said out loud. He had meant to keep it to himself. But it didn't matter that it slipped out.

Pesty looked at him hard. "Oh, you mean . . ."

"Yeah," he said. "About your mama and Mr. Pluto and their discovery."

"How it's not true," she said.

"The real secret is that we've known about the cavern for a long time and kept it from your father and the foundation."

"And Mr. Pluto knew the longest," she said. "I sure hated keeping it from Daddy."

"Do you know why your mama kept the underground rooms from him?" he asked.

"My daddy has a way of taking over things," she said.

"Well, your mama sure didn't keep the great cavern from your daddy," Thomas said.

"No, she didn't ever know about that," Pesty said. "Mr. Pluto told me never to tell anyone about that, so I didn't."

"Ump, ump, ump," Thomas murmured. "You were just such a little girl when you first knew about the cavern. I guess maybe that's why you could keep it in. Some little kids are like that. You kept it this long; you should be proud. It's all sure something!"

"Yeah, and my brothers are mad they didn't get their pictures taken."

"Macky, too?"

"Macky the most," she said. "He acts like he thinks you and me *planned* to get famous. He's been asking me when I'm going to see you. Like he wants me to ask him to come along." She waited for Thomas to say something.

He'd almost given up on Macky, but down deep he still had a little hope left. A little place saved for friendship.

It was said that Drear treasure was worth millions.

They were even on cable television. There was Thomas's papa on the six o'clock news, shown in his office in the college and, next, explaining about the treasure from inside the cavern. The history of everything. There were shots of the house of Dies Drear, Thomas's own home. Thomas couldn't believe it. Television trucks and people all over the place. And the whole town and everybody for miles seeing them, too.

"That's really me!" Thomas had said.

It had been reported that there would be a reward for Mrs. Darrow and Mr. Skinner but that the foundation wouldn't say how much. River Lewis got to talk about his family and how they knew there had to be treasure.

"Your daddy still keeping the reward amount a secret?" Thomas asked.

"Yeah," she said. "Guess he has to have his own secret."

Thomas sighed. "Wish we could ask Mr. Pluto. But Papa says you just don't ask someone how much they got for something."

"I don't see why," Pesty said. "Anyway, I already know."

"Pesty, you do? Tell me!" Thomas exclaimed.

"I found out just last night," she said.

"Well . . ." He was going to say, "Well, how much?" But then he thought about what his papa had said. Somebody would tell you only if that person wanted to.

She grinned at him. Leaning very close to his ear, she whispered.

"*Ten thousand dollars?*" He mouthed the words silently.

"Uh-huh," she said, talking softly. "Daddy told it to Mama. They brought around a check for her. I was in the closet; I had to wait until Daddy left."

That's another secret, Thomas thought fleetingly. His papa had never told the foundation or River Lewis, either, about the way from Mattie's bedroom to the underground rooms. "Let them discover it for themselves. See how long it takes *them*. Maybe forever," his papa had said. It hurt his papa, too, to give up everything to what he called posterity.

"Ten thousand dollars!" Thomas whispered. "And then Mr. Pluto . . ."

"Uh-huh, he got the same," she said. "They sure bring a fast reward!"

"That makes . . . twenty thousand dollars the foundation gave. Wow! Is your daddy happy?" Thomas asked.

"Well, he don't appear to be too sad," she said. "He's fearsome, though, about having lost the great cavern. And all his whole family looking for it. But a bird in hand—the ten thousand . . ."

"Yeah," Thomas said. "The ten thousand's a sure thing."

Thomas got up, shook the snow off. "We'd better get going if we're going over," he said.

"Okay," Pesty said. She put the blanket down in the

bare spot where she'd been sitting. Then they started out. "It's a wonderland," she added. The trees were wet and dark, etched in white snow lines.

"Be Thanksgiving soon, too," Thomas said.

They reached the clearing in front of Mr. Pluto's. There they saw the two guards who had been inside Pluto's cave entrance since just after THE EVENT had taken place. Now, there was a semitruck, an enormous eighteen-wheeler, pulled up to the cave entrance. Men were busy hauling out the treasure of Dies Drear.

They walked around the back of the semi to get to the front of the cave, out of the way of the movers. Thomas saw Mayhew's car with a trailer attached.

"What is this?" He wondered out loud.

They came up to the guards and were recognized. "Can we get by, see Mr. Pluto?" Thomas asked. It felt funny, having to ask. But the men said yes, letting them in.

Thomas had thought it was foolish, at first, that the foundation went to the trouble to post guards. But then his papa had said, "All that publicity, too many folks would like to just walk in, take a few souvenirs."

"People really would do that?" Thomas had asked.

"It's human nature," his papa had said.

Inside the cave they found Mayhew and Pluto. They were over on the side, out of the way of the treasure parade from the cavern. Thomas looked around, speechless. The portable forge was nowhere to be seen. All of Pluto's pictures on the walls and even the yellowed calendars had been packed up. There was no table, no carpet. His comfortable brass bed, the worn armchair, his bathrobe, pots and pans had been moved out.

Mayhew stood looking at Thomas and Pesty as they came in. Tiredly he waved at them in greeting but didn't say anything. Mr. Pluto sat on the one straight chair. Pluto had on his best Sunday suit and his familiar black dress cape and high hat. Bent over like an old man, he held his brown throw tightly about him over the cape. His eyes clouded over as Thomas came up to him. "I can't take my Josie," he said forlornly, talking about his horse. It was the saddest thing Thomas had ever heard.

"You can't take Josie where?" Thomas said, alarmed. "Mr. Pluto, where are you going? Mayhew, what's happening?"

"Thomas, they're going to be moving stuff out of here for days. Tramping through with mud, the doors wide open," Mayhew said. "He can't live with that."

"But where are you taking him?" Thomas said.

"He's going to move to town," Mayhew said. "I found an apartment for him that the senior citizens' organization provides for the elderly."

"Aw, pshaw!" Mr. Pluto muttered in disgust.

"Well, what else can I do?" Mayhew said, spreading empty hands. "I'll stay around until he's settled. He's going to enjoy it more than he thinks, aren't you, Father?"

Pesty came over, leaned her head on Pluto's shoulder, the way she always had.

Mr. Pluto rested his head against hers. Gently he said, "Son, don't think I don't appreciate all you've done for me. He worked hard all morning, he taken everything on his shoulders"—this last, directed to Pesty and Thomas. "Said he wanted to do it all hisself."

They heard somebody come in. Thomas glanced around to see. "Papa!" There were his papa and mama. "Well, I'll be!" Thomas said. "I didn't know you guys were coming over here." They were dressed for the cold. His mama had high boots on.

"Have to give the foundation some more of my inventory," Mr. Small said, waving a clipboard and a folder stuffed with papers at Thomas.

"Are they already down there?" Thomas asked. He walked over to see. People from the foundation were sure down there.

"I think they probably stayed the night," his papa said.

"They did," Mayhew said. "They sent out for breakfast, too."

"Goodness," Mrs. Small said.

"Morning, y'all," Pesty said, glad to see them.

"Hi, there, girl!" Mrs. Small said. "Hello, Mayhew! How are you feeling today, Mr. Skinner?" she said, using Pluto's proper last name.

"Oh well . . ." he said, but said no more.

Just by looking, Martha Small could tell how he felt. "Did you-all find a place in town?"

"Senior citizens," Pluto murmured. "I guess I'm old now."

"Father, it doesn't mean you're old to move into the senior citizens."

"Yes, it does," Pesty said.

"Little Miss Bee knows," Pluto said. "Senior can't take care of hisself."

"All right now," Mr. Small said. "We can't have this. Look, Mayhew, Henry." Walter Small knelt beside Pluto's chair. "There really is no need for this. I don't know why I didn't say something before. It's been vague in the back of my mind. And you know, we wouldn't want to interfere. I've been so busy. Henry, listen to me. There's no reason at all that you have to go into town. What about our house? I mean, what about living with us?"

There was a moment's silence. Mr. Pluto lifted his head. "Oh, I couldn't do a thing like that, no, no. I won't be a burden to anyone."

"Who says you'd be a burden?" Martha Small said. "Why, it's a wonderful idea. Great-grandmother is here. And you two really do get along! And the twins, why, they adore you."

"Well I'll be . . ." Thomas said. Things change before your very eyes! "It's really a big place. You'll just love it," he said eagerly to Pluto. "It's the best ol' house for sleeping! You can take the twins and Great-grandmother for buggy rides." He grinned from ear to ear.

22

Thanksgiving came and went. It had been foggy and rainy the whole day. Mr. Pluto and Mayhew were at the Smalls' Thanksgiving dinner, and Pesty, too. Afterward Thomas's mama sent turkey and stuffing and pie home with Pesty. Thomas helped Pesty carry everything. It was all right that he hadn't been asked to come into Pesty's house. He wasn't sure he would want to go in. He had left what he carried at the Darrow front door, he told his mama.

There should have been snow on Thanksgiving, too, and sleigh bells in his head, as there were today. Sure glad today is all right, he thought. It snowed every day now. And this, another Sunday, was a snowy Sunday.

Everybody's at my house, he thought. He couldn't quite believe it. He felt weak, having spent his energy on not acting dumb. Right and wrong were so close together in the same house, for the first time. My house!

Smalls and Darrows, Pluto. Mayhew had left town to go back to his work after Thanksgiving, after settling Pluto in. Thomas didn't know whose idea it had been to invite Darrows over for this Sunday dinner. Probably his mama's. Both his mama and his papa had agreed on it.

Love thy neighbor! Thomas thought scornfully.

Darrows dared accept the invitation and had driven up in cars.

Thomas could hardly believe it. I mean, River Lewis Darrow and his boys and Macky, and Pesty, of course, and Mrs. Darrow, Thomas thought. And Mama and Papa, Billy and Buster and Great-grandmother. Plus Mr. Pluto. In the kitchen. In the parlor. All fourteen of us.

And Mr. Pluto living with us and settled in, Thomas went on. Well, it had taken awhile to convince him. But it's something to hear him on the stairs in the morning! He and Great-grandmother Jeffers talking all the time, busy at things. The twins get a buggy ride each day.

And I bet Pesty will just move in one day. She sleeps over some of the time already.

Look at it snow! Thomas sat there in the parlor in a straight chair next to the fireplace, facing Darrows. He had been looking out the long windows to calm himself. He thought about the only one who was missing: Mayhew Skinner. Mayhew had refused to come back to eat with Darrows. He'd be civil to them from a distance, he'd said over the phone, but he wasn't going out of his way. Thank you anyhow.

Glad he hasn't changed, Thomas thought. Maybe it's good that somebody remembers what Darrows were once and might still be.

"About ten da-grees above," he heard River Lewis Darrows tell Great-grandmother Jeffers, concerning the weather. Her voice tinkled back at him.

River Lewis Darrow's tone was deep and bold, like formal bell rings, talking to his sons or Great-grandmother or Mattie. His was a cold sound to match his pearl gray Sunday suit. He was formal and stiff, just barely on the decent side of unfriendly the whole time he was in the house. Gruff out of habit. He couldn't sit down but stood, a barrier to all concerned.

Mattie Darrow had refused sitting at the table that had been set. She had become agitated when anybody else tried to sit down. "She wants that set-up table to stay like a picture right where it is," River Lewis said. He did not apologize for Mattie. He reached out with one hand and let his fingers touch her hair. "Miz

Small, Mistah Small," he said, looking down at the floor. "Mattie, glad ta be here. All us, too."

Well, you sure don't act like it, Thomas thought.

"We are certainly glad you all could come, and welcome!" Mrs. Small said, smiling warmly. "Come on, everybody, let's all have a good time."

Mattie then chose by herself where she would sit. "It doesn't make a bit of difference where we eat," Mrs. Small murmured.

Who knows the reason why Mattie Darrow is the way she is? Thomas thought.

His mama set the dinner as a buffet. Chicken and stuffing, potatoes, coleslaw, gravy. There were two baked ducks the Darrows had brought, which seemed out of place on an ordinary Sunday.

When was the last time I tasted duck? Thomas thought.

They all served themselves from the kitchen table. River Lewis kept his clumsy sons in line. When they filled their plates to heaping, he gave them a look, and they walked away from the table. When it was time for seconds, he stood by, staring hard at them. Wilbur, Russell, and River Ross Darrow were as meek as little lambs, pouring themselves milk or sparkling cider.

Whenever Thomas's papa walked into the room to offer River Lewis some extra main course or fill his glass, Darrow backed up a pace or two. Now he was straight against the wall across from the parlor fireplace. Mattie sat on a cushioned footrest next to him.

And beside her sat Great-grandmother, with the two little fellows in their rocking chairs right by their knees. Great-grandmother and Mattie were feeding the twins expertly. Billy and Buster didn't find it odd that River Lewis was guarding the wall. Or that Mattie Darrow sometimes stared fiercely around, cackling.

All of them were in the parlor now. Thomas, Pesty, and Macky had fixed their plates right after the grown-ups. Pesty, Mrs. Small, and Mr. Pluto shared the parlor couch. Pesty was closest to Thomas. Mr. Small leaned against the wall next to River Lewis. Darrow's sons moved away to make room for him. Once the sons were over being scared, they looked only halfway uncomfortable. But they ate everything in sight, Thomas noted, amused.

Thomas had a full plate of dinner in one hand and a warm roll in a yellow linen napkin on his knees. A glass of sparkling cider was next to his feet. His polished Sunday shoes weren't scuffed yet. He had a fork in the other hand. Thomas could eat, chew. But he probably wouldn't enjoy eating until he could eat the leftovers out of the refrigerator, after everybody *strange* had gone home.

"Macky, you bagged the ducks?" Mr. Small asked, commenting how good they were.

"Yes."

"Yes, sir." River Lewis corrected him, not unkindly, it seemed to Thomas.

"Yes . . . sir." Macky looked surprised that his father

had spoken to him. And he answered carefully to Mr. Small. "I brought them down as they went over— ducks like to fly from pond to pond around here."

"He shot 'em clean," River Lewis said. And Macky looked as if he would go through the ceiling from happiness.

All of us, looking nice, Thomas commented to himself. First time I've seen Pesty's hair combed since the last Sunday at church, he thought. He told her it looked nice.

"Macky combed it. Mama told him how," she told Thomas.

"Oh, girl!" Macky muttered.

Thomas smiled at him, to show him he understood how his mama's hands might not always work right.

Macky sat on the other side of the hot fireplace from Thomas. "Looks like a department store in here," Macky commented, talking about how dressed up they all were. That had broken the ice between him and Thomas. Made Thomas almost choke with the giggles. The two of them, big guys together. He unbuttoned his jacket and vest just the way Macky had. This was some Sunday! All dressed up together and nowhere to go.

Mr. Small made conversation as best he could. Rumors about Darrows were all over town and the college. Not just about the ten thousand dollars River Lewis and Mr. Pluto, too, had gotten. Rumor said that River Lewis had been hired by the foundation to show them the underground, all of it that he knew and his family had known over time.

As if on cue, River Lewis spoke. "Foundation given me a good job." And partly unwillingly, he added, "I be thanking you for that, Mr. Small."

Later Thomas and his papa found themselves in the kitchen alone, preparing coffee and coffee cake. Thomas waited for the dessert to warm up in a slow oven. He and his papa talked privately. "When the contents of the great cavern and the underground rooms are removed," his papa said, "the cavern and the rooms are to be replicated. There is to be a museum for the Drear collections."

"What does 'replicated' mean?" Thomas asked.

"It means to re-create," his papa said. "The foundation will reproduce the cavern and the rooms on a smaller scale. And it will put back some of the treasure and the other things in the display."

"Wow!" whispered Thomas.

"Yes, and the whole lot will look like a real underground, like the originals," his papa said. "They might even have a figure of Drear at the desk, if they want to hoke it up a little. Then the museum will open to the public."

"They'll probably hire Pesty to play an orphan child," Thomas said, half joking and half angry.

"Thomas, that isn't nice."

"Well, I don't think it's fair," Thomas said. "They gave River Lewis a job. They gave him money. And even a couple of the gold triangles. That's what everybody is saying anyway."

"It's up to the foundation to decide what it wants to give River Lewis," Mr. Small said. "Who knows the countryside better than he? But they have asked him not to farm the land until they've emptied the underground."

"Darrows have a brand-new pickup truck," Thomas said. "And River Lewis has a new car. And his big old sons have a new jeep!"

"Keep your voice down," Mr. Small told him. "Thomas, how can you resent their coming up in the world when they had nothing?"

"But it isn't fair! What did *you* get?" he said.

"Oh, I see," his papa said. "Well, I'm still cataloging everything, Thomas. And before there can be a museum, I'll have to record the history of those rooms down there and all about the orphan children and the heroine, the Indian maiden. The foundation will pay me for my work, too."

"I bet not as much as River Lewis gets," Thomas said.

"Thomas, Thomas!" Mr. Small sighed and put his arm around Thomas. "Son, I'm a historian. I'm happy to save a great discovery from its worst enemies—time and greed. I've held the 'villain' in check. I've shown him I care about his welfare, and treat him like a friend. I've managed to help give him the possibility of a better lifetime. At least, to give him an even chance.

Do you understand? And what River Lewis does with
the rest of his days is up to him. And what you do with
yours, Thomas, and Macky with his, is up to the both
of you."

Friend. Caring. Friend or foe? he wondered about
himself and Macky.

Back in the parlor he had a piece of the cake and
more cider. He felt Macky looking at him. Macky
reached over and poked him in his arm. "Let's get out
of here," he said, just slightly above the sound of the
strained talking around them.

"Okay," Thomas said as coolly as he could.

"Me, too?" Pesty leaned toward them, smiling at her
brother.

"Yeah," Macky murmured, "you, too, I guess."

The three of them got up, hands full of plates,
glasses, napkins. Macky went over to stand before
River Lewis. "Daddy," Macky said politely, "we wanting
to go outside now."

"Oh, that's a good idea," Great-grandmother said,
smiling. "You-all walk around in the fresh air a few
minutes, you'll feel like my pumpkin pie!" She smiled
at Macky and his father. "That coffee cake was just the
appetizer!"

"Macs," Mattie Darrow said, smacking her lips, "get
more glass." She held up her empty cider glass.

"I'll get it for you," River Lewis said. He nodded at
Macky. "Find Pesty's coat for her then. She don't never
want to wear a coat." He lifted his voice, saying that.

Looking around, including everybody in what he'd said. Thomas realized River Lewis wanted them to know that he had bought Pesty a new coat. "She grows so fast," he added as Thomas and Macky came back in with just scarves and gloves on. Pesty had on her new velvet-looking coat. It was awfully pretty, Thomas thought, with gold buttons and a velvet hat to match. She certainly had needed a new coat. She stood in front of River Lewis as Mattie raised her hands to her.

"She wants you to button the top button," River Lewis said, speaking for Mattie. Mattie touched Pesty's gloved hands. "Says, 'Don't get too cold, don't stay out too long,'" he added.

"I won't," Pesty said, her eyes shining. She took a deep breath of happiness, gave her mama a big hug, and buttoned her top coat button. She gave River Lewis a loving look. And this time he bowed to her just slightly. That small touch of respect spoke through his gruffness. Not only "things" were different. He does care, Thomas couldn't help thinking.

"You look so pretty, Pesty," Mrs. Small said. "That's a beautiful coat."

"Thank you," she said.

River Lewis looked stern but proud.

Outside, it was cold. But it was better than the oppressive, uncomfortable scene inside. "I hope I don't have to go through that again soon," Martha Small was to say later.

"They were trying very hard," Great-grandmother said, and Walter Small had agreed.

Thomas and Macky and Pesty walked around the house on the veranda. Thomas shivered. It still snowed. They leaned against the outside wall of the veranda between the long window and the front door. Pesty was in the middle. For a time they didn't speak. Then, suddenly, Macky said, "Everybody talking to me, talking about how we rich. Shoot. We ain't rich." He laughed contemptuously. "We just now gettin' what everybody else *been* having."

"I . . . guess that's true," Thomas said. "What—what did the foundation give you all? I mean, there are such rumors."

"I don't want to talk about it," he said resentfully. "Everybody lying so."

"Because he don't know what they give Daddy besides a job. Daddy don't tell nobody," Pesty said.

"Did they give him some triangles?" Thomas said.

"I said . . ." Macky spoke but didn't finish. He sounded angry.

"Okay then," Thomas said. He went tight inside as he said to Macky through his teeth. "It was you in Mr. Pluto's cave, wasn't it?"

"Yeah, it was." Pesty piped up.

"I can speak for myself!" Macky said, raising a hand to her.

"Mr. Pluto said you wasn't to bother me!" she said, cringing toward Thomas.

"I'm not *touching* you. I'm not *studying* you!" Macky said. He let his hand drop. "Girl! I just can speak for *myself*." He hung his head and was silent a long time. "Don't tell anybody," he said finally, looking at Thomas.

"It's—it's over now," Thomas said.

"I was just hoping . . ."

"I know," Thomas said.

"But that's not all," Macky said. He looked away.

"What then?" Thomas asked.

"Mama," he said. "Worried about her doing something, didn't know what. Didn't want you-all Smalls to see her like she was." He swallowed hard.

"Lots of people can get sick like her," Thomas said.

"Well, I didn't know you would think that," Macky said softly.

"You and Pesty had the same idea," Thomas said.

"How's that?" Macky said.

"Because your mama was sick and your daddy was mad at you, you wanted to hurry and find treasure maybe to make it all better. That's why you went . . . to Mr. Pluto's. Pesty wanted the same thing, kind of, because your mama was in the tunnels and in our house. She was afraid we'd see your mama or she'd get hurt, what all. But you didn't know that there is a tunnel from your house to the underground."

"No, I didn't know that," Macky said. "There is?"

"Mama's closet opens to a tunnel," Pesty said. "She love the orphan place and to sit in the parlor room down there. You better come see it before they empty it. Once they empty it, maybe we can fix it up for her a little. Mr. Small never did tell the foundation about that closet opening. You can tell Daddy if you want. Just don't tell him I knew about it."

Macky looked stunned.

"If you tell your dad about the tunnel from your house to Drear house," Thomas said, puzzling it out, "well, he can tell the foundation."

"And that'll make Daddy real happy, because of you!" Pesty told him. "And he'll look real good to the foundation. And everybody will know about everything."

Macky nodded. "Thanks!" he said to both of them. He was silent again, looking at his feet, before he said, "Mama shouldn'ta been in the tunnels. It kept her down in an unreal world. I never want to see the place!" He'd seen the orphans' room and the parlor room on television, and that was enough.

"Mama likes it down there," Pesty said.

"Still," Macky said, "it must've kept her too much in the past."

"We should know about the past," Thomas said, "but we shouldn't let the past take us over."

"You can't live in it," Macky said. "We got to try to change Mama's mind about that."

"Man, do things turn around fast!" Thomas said.

Macky shook his head with the mystery of it all. He walked to the edge of the veranda, stuck his face out, and looked up at the falling snow. It fell into his eyes. "Feels like I'm rising up," he said.

Pesty followed and leaned her head out. "Just does feel like I'm uprising, too," she said.

"It makes you dizzy," Thomas said, coming over. He looked up, felt himself lifted into the snowflakes at a dizzying speed.

"Now what you think you-all doing?" Mr. Pluto said, coming out on the veranda. Nothing on his shoulders but his shirtsleeves. "Brrrr! Come on, they say it's time for punkun pie and whip cream."

"Oh, goody!" Pesty said.

"Look at it snow!" Mr. Pluto said. "Glad I don't have to go home this night. Ha! Already home. Home with Mr. Drear, in his house! Ain't that something?"

Thomas laughed, clearly seeing the past linked to the present: the Drear house alive with the living; all past struggles and troubles brought to light in the present. He nudged Macky as Pesty and Mr. Pluto went back inside. "Ghosts!" he murmured. They both laughed.

"You want to hunt tomorrow?" Macky asked him.

"Will the snow stop?"

"Might by then," Macky said. "We'll have to go farther out, off Drear land. And our land. The foundation folks want no hunting near or on their grounds."

"Really?" Thomas said. "We can go as far as you want, after school."

"Then, on Saturday, we can hunt all day." Macky said.

Thomas felt his heart leap. "Okay!" he said.

He would follow Macky. Let him find a trail of something. Or let him shoot first, out over a pond somewhere—see how he bagged his birds.

I'll bring some sandwiches, Thomas thought. And ice skates! Let him lead. For a while. It'll be a long winter. Somewhere in it I'll lead.

Friends take turns. He grinned like a kid at Macky's broad back.

They went inside where it was warm.